ANGEL STEEL

RANDY CHANDLER

RED ROOM PRESS

RED ROOM PRESS

"Chandler again demonstrates his mastery at telling solid, horrific tales—in this case, a dark and mysterious modern passion play with demons and even more terrifying angels. Randy Chandler is a name to be remembered and read!"

—Gregory L. Norris, *Shrunken Heads: 20 Tiny Tales of Mystery and Terror*

A JOURNEY OF DARKNESS BEGINS

Without hesitation, she accepts the radiant sword. It has little weight and she wields it with astounding ease. The sword's dark power courses through the deeper channels of her soul, and she truly believes she is tasting immortality. Glimpses of other worlds and Heavenly dimensions flash before her. A sharp edge of bright awareness prevents her from becoming drunk with the sword's awesome power.

Rahab was right. She would follow him and his bewitching blade anywhere, even into the innards of Hell. And beyond.

ALSO BY RANDY CHANDLER

NOVELS AND COLLECTIONS:

Daemon of the Dark Wood

Devils, Death & Dark Wonders

Dime Detective

Duet for the Devil (with t. winter-damon)

Hellz Bellz

Bad Juju

Stolen Roads

EDITOR:

Stiff Things: The Splatterporn Anthology

Red Room Magazine

Year's Best Hardcore Horror

TABLE OF CONTENTS

ANGEL STEEL

7

BONUS STORY

RORC

149

I. THE VISIONARY

Brother Thomas paced the stone floor of his cell, keeping to the darkened corners and avoiding the skeletal fingers of yellow light fluttering from the single candle beside his cot. As much as the light terrified him, the darkness frightened him more, so he could not simply walk over to the candle and pinch out the flame with licked-wet fingers. That a monastic brother should be so cursed with a fear of light seemed an affront to Thomas's religious calling, but he could find no remedy for it.

The visions always came with a burst of painful light no one else could see, with the agonizing sensation of talons hooking his head and piercing his cranium to unleash a terrible shrieking within. The insufferably luminous visitations inevitably left him with an illogical fear of light—and with the certainty that his spirit was withering, twisting into some Hellish deformity that not even God would recognize as a soul.

As his bare feet whispered over the floor, he beseeched the Lord to spare him the torment of further visions. He did not believe he could survive another. But even as he addressed the Almighty with his desperate petition, fear inflamed his soul and he broke off his prayer. It was then he knew that he feared God more than he feared the darkness and the light. The shameful impulse to hide from God, to become invisible, drove him to crouch in the darkest corner of his austere cell, where he trembled like a newborn calf. In his mind's eye he saw the Lord's fiery finger burning away the ceiling of the small room and pointing directly at him, singling him out from his brethren in the monastery, designating this weak, unworthy monk as the recipient of insidious visions.

"O Lord…" he cried. "No more."

Unseen talons dug into his skull. Screaming, he jumped to his feet and bolted from his cell, clutching his head in his hands as if to hold it in place on his thin neck and narrow shoulders. Down the dim corridor he ran, alternately whimpering and mouthing delirious imprecations. He brushed past brothers who had stumbled, sleep-befuddled, from their cells to see what the matter was, and then he loped up the staircase and out into the snow-covered courtyard. There he dropped to his knees, pressed his palms together as if preparing to pray, and then he wordlessly screamed at the Heavens until his throat was too raw to scream more.

The terrible shrieking filled his skull, and like a bellows stoking flames, the shrieking brought forth the vision that filled him with mortal terror and revulsion.

Great white wings come out of the heavy snowfall, winged creatures silently gliding toward the earth, brandishing fiery blades.

Hideous giants and fearsome demons with otherworldly weapons rise up to meet their airborne enemy. Battle blades rend the cold air, clashing with steel thunder.

The snow burns red with bloodfall.

Stricken angels crash to earth. Others strive to escape on damaged wings.

Above the battle, an immense and angry God curses the world and turns away in disgust. Untouched by the raging combat, Thomas wanders for a time on bloody fields of snow, and then he is all at once hurled backward in time to witness the cause of this unholy slaughter.

What he sees drives him deeper into madness.

He fell forward into the deep snow and into the yawning darkness beneath it. His brothers carried him back into the monastery, where he languished feverishly for three days between life and death, between this world and the next, tormented by ungodly visions.

When at last he came out of his fever, he shouted: "Something terrible is coming into the world!"

II. SONG OF BIRTH AND DEATH

Braga's mother often sang a womb-song to her before she was born, but once she had squeezed the infant out into the cold world, the weary mother never again sang that childbearing song. When the girl-child was old enough to understand, her mother told her that their people would sing glorious songs of Braga's heroic exploits down the long chain of time and that she would be remembered long after her era on earth was done. She told Braga, too, that she would hear the womb-song once more, that she would recognize it at once and know it signaled her mother's death. "But mother," the youngster puzzled in her childish way, "how can I know a song you sang before you borned me, a song I never heard?" To which her mother replied: "You *did* hear it, little one. You heard it with your spirit before you had ears, and you heard it again with your tiny ears through the waters of my womb. You will know the song when the spirit-wind brings it to your ears. Have no fear."

And now, twenty-two years after her birth, alone under a full moon on a mist-cloaked moor in the low country of the south, Braga heard the prophesied song again and knew her mother was dying. She lifted her helm off her war-braids, halted her great mount and cocked her ears to the faint music the spirit-wind carried. Her heavy breasts heaved beneath her hard-hide breastplate. Her eyes moistened with mists of sadness. Before she refitted the moon-hazed helm upon her head and turned her horse for home, she uttered one word: "Mother."

Just before rosy dawn Braga rode hard into the village and jumped down from her mount before the horse's hooves ceased pounding ground. Her long legs carried her on the run to her mother's hut. The woman, now aged and frost-headed by many hard winters, looked up with rheumy eyes at her sturdy daughter and tried to smile. The old woman's face was badly bruised and battered, one eye swollen shut and the lower lip split open.

"Mother, who did this to you?" Braga asked, struggling to keep her voice gentle.

Her mother averted her one visible eye, but nevertheless hazarded an answer. Something broken rattled in her chest as she spoke. "Nathor of the Nephs. Caught me by the stream. Thrashed me. He stopped short of killing me outright 'cause he wanted me alive long enough for you to come home to me one last time."

"I'll kill him!" Braga roared. Her long war-braids shook like angry serpents beneath her helm.

"That's why he did this. He wants you to come to him."

"I won't disappoint the monster!" Braga clutched the haft of her sheathed sword. "I'll have his head on a pike."

"Kneel by me, daughter." The dying woman weakly extended her gnarled hand. Braga knelt by the deathbed, removed her helmet and took her mother's hand. The old woman whispered, "Nathor wants you because…he is your true father."

Braga dropped the withered hand as if it were a fiery brand. Anger blazed in her eyes. Then she softened her aspect and took up the old hand again, saying, "The blows to your head addled your brain, otherwise you wouldn't speak such nonsense."

"No, my daughter, it's true. Twenty-three years ago Nathor killed my husband, ripped open my loins and assaulted my womanhood. It nearly tore me apart, but I was big and strong then. You're the spawn of the foul giant. You must tell no one this, as I have kept my silence 'till now. Have you never wondered why you were so much taller and stronger than even the men of our tribe? Why you've grown into such a fierce warrior? It's his blood in your veins."

"Then why am I not as hideous as those man-killing monsters?"

"You took your beauty from my mother, the fairest of our tribe."

Braga laughed bitterly. "So Nathor wants to be a father to me now? To bounce me on his knee? Tell me stories of his race of fiends? How can I believe this madness?"

"He wants you to carry his child," rasped the old woman, her frail voice growing weaker still, "so your prowess and beauty might be bred into his bloodline."

"He told you this?"

"No. I read it in his ugly face, in his bulging eyes."

"I'll have off his manhood before I lop off his ugly head," Braga said through clenched teeth.

"You must not go near him. Nathor is cunning. He'll keep you penned up like a pregnant sow until you birth him a child. Then he will likely kill you."

Braga kissed her mother's cheek. "Don't tire yourself with worry.

Rest now. By the time of the new moon you will be your crabby old self again."

Sadness filled the old woman's eyes, and Braga saw in them death and foreknowledge of death, and she knew her mother would not live to see the day's sunset, much less the new moon.

Then with great effort the old woman spoke her last words to her daughter: "There is no shame in your dark heritage. In making you, the Great Mother took the strengths of that foul race of giants and made them human, fashioned them into something new and wonderful. My Braga…" Thereupon, she closed her eyes and drifted for a time in the nether regions between this world and the next.

Braga heard stir of movement—a rustle of wings?—behind her and spun round with her hand on the dagger she wore on her left side. She relaxed when she saw her little tow-headed cousin Tyka clutching her pet chicken. The child's eyes were wide and wet with innocent concern for the fatally injured old woman. The bird's eyes were beady, dulled by such close captivity. Tyka whimpered.

Braga held her finger to her lips to shush the girl, then gently led her out of the hut.

"Is Gran dying?" asked Tyka, lips quivering.

"Yes, she's resting for her journey to the next world."

"Can I go with her?" Tyka clutched the chicken tighter. The helpless bird squawked.

"No. She has to go alone. And you have to stay here to grow up and try to be as good a woman as your Gran. Think you can do that?"

The child nodded. Braga tousled Tyka's hair and sent her back to her hut, where the child's mother would be preparing breakfast.

Braga gathered her two and twenty warriors together under the council tree, a giant oak with thick winter arms reaching into the early-morning sky. The strapping younger men were eager to take revenge on her mother's assailant, though none yet knew the culprit's identity. The more seasoned fighters kept a thoughtful silence and closely watched their arresting leader.

She seized the painted council stick and raised it over her head to signal her readiness to address her men. When their blustering subsided, she spoke: "I need three men to ride with me. The rest of you will stay here to guard the village. Sek, Mulki, and Taboor—you will come with me. The rest of you, be vigilant. The Nephs are close by. And the Wulfangs have returned to their winter camp and are ever a threat to us. No man sleeps tonight."

"Who did this terrible thing to your mother?" asked Gragor, the band's brashest young warrior.

"Nathor of the Nephs," she said. "He is not your worry. I'll deal his death myself."

Gragor stepped forward, brandishing his long spear. "Then I should go with you," he said. "You can't best the Nephs with three old men."

Taboor one-handed his bludgeon and knocked the younger man's legs out from under him, and then put his foot on Gragor's throat and hawked a wad of spit into the upstart's face. With a wide grin splitting his wild beard Taboor said, "This old man will crack your skull and spill your brains if you don't show proper respect, stripling. Now get off your arse and apologize to our lady."

Before the red-faced grounded man could get up, Braga said, "I want no apologies. Just follow your orders and stay alive through the night when it comes." Then to the chosen three she said, "Make ready. We leave before the sun's shadow touches the blue stone."

As Braga strode on long legs to her own small hut, her mother's gray-haired nurse intercepted her and said, "Your mother's gone."

Braga bit back an upwelling of emotion and nodded. "Any last words?"

"No. Death rattled her spirit free and then she passed over quietly."

"Bury her before the sun sinks." Braga said as she glanced at her mother's tiny hut and saw Tyka standing in its doorway, peering inside at the cooling corpse. A single tear escaped Braga's eye and she silently cursed herself for showing weakness. Little Tyka began to whine like a lost puppy.

Braga strode across the cold ground to the crying child, snatched the pet chicken from her tiny arms and wrenched off the bird's head.

"Stop your sniveling, child," Braga said. "You must learn to let go of worldly things."

III. RAGE IN HEAVEN

When Rahab could no longer suffer the love of God, his rage resounded within the vaulting halls of sidereal crystal, and his fierce aspect sowed dissonance within the hierarchical choir. The harmonious wheel of the many-eyed ones hummed with alarm, fearful that prideful Rahab would arouse God's wrath.

Rahab laughed bitterly at the fearful kowtowers, then stormed off to the very edge of Heaven, where he thought he might breathe the nourishing light afresh, away from the suffocating sameness of celestial existence.

Presently, Melchizedek the Prince of Light approached him with his wise counsel, but Rahab would have none of it. "I have not the heart anymore for the Lord's enslaving love," Rahab said. "I yearn to be free of it, to go down into the world of men and drink my fill of cruel freedom and to know sin firsthand. All this Heavenly devotion is meaningless if I am not tested in the violent world of Man. If I remain here, this pent-up rage will destroy me."

"Father would not allow that to happen," Melchizedek told him.

Rahab's sardonic laughter crackled like lightning. "No," he said, "the Father would cast me out before it came to that. But I will not give Him the chance, my brother. I shall cast myself from this insufferable place, to rise again on my own merit or sink into eternal Damnation. Farewell!"

And with that, Rahab plunged into the atmospheres of time, soared above the earthly plane, and then translated himself into the chaotic world of men, souls and sin.

IV. BATTLE FURY

The ground was laced with week-old snow, making it easy to follow Nathor's big clubfooted tracks away from the stream where the behemoth had fatally pounded Braga's mother. The sun was sinking through layers of purple clouds toward the horizon as Braga and her three warriors rode at as brisk a pace as tracking would allow.

Taboor canted his mount close beside hers and said, "You know we're riding into a trap."

"We've dared them before," she reminded him, "and we've never been caught in the trap's teeth."

"This time could be different." A scowl rode the weathered prow of his face. "We've never taken down a Neph in battle. We've avoided them like the pox for years and with good reason. I'd have to stand on the shoulders of two tall men to bash one's skull."

"I'll chop him down for you." She touched the haft of the long sword she wore on her back. Her face was grim, anger still seething in her chest.

Taboor grumbled wordlessly. Sek rode ahead, as he was the skilled tracker. A longbow hanging off his shoulder, Mulki rode slightly behind, guarding their flank.

Turning inexplicably pensive, Braga said, "Those of the Cult of the Cross say the messengers of their god once mated with mortal women and spawned a race of evil giants that their god destroyed with a great flood. The messengers were called *mal'akh,* what some call angels."

"You don't believe that dung," said Taboor. "Do you?"

She shrugged. "If it's true, they got the story's ending wrong. Some of those giants must've found high ground to survive the flood. The Nephs are evil giants—that much we know for true."

"*Mal'akh,*" Taboor said, tasting the strange word on his tongue. "How do you know so much about this?"

"When I was a child, Mother and I met a wandering Brew of the Lost Tribe of Rael in the river-town of Ox Ford," she said. "Mother always liked to talk to strangers, especially men with knowledge of the gods, and I was all ears back then."

"All ears and remembering," he said with a rumbling chuckle. "I don't know how you have room for it all in your pretty little head."

She shot him a look of displeasure. He ignored it and went on: "The pictures I've seen of angels show them as fat little babies with fluttering wings or as womanish men. They don't look like they could sprout a lick of iron from their loins, much less father a race of giants."

"There are different kinds, they say. Some are fiery avengers with flaming swords."

"*That's* the kind I'd like to see," Taboor said. "I would trade my bludgeon and two hogs for one of *those* swords."

Up ahead, Sek halted and pointed with his spear at something in their path. "Fresh scat," he said over his shoulder.

The others rode up even with him and looked down at the heap of stinking dung.

"Gods, but that's the foulest shit I've ever smelled," said Taboor.

Sek dismounted and squatted beside the knee-high pile of droppings. He picked up a stick and poked the mound of squashy brown filth.

"Ughh, I hate when he does that," Taboor said, spitting.

Braga cupped her hand over her nose and mouth to blunt the stench. Gagging, Mulki walked his mount several steps backward.

Sek dug something out of the shit and held it up on the end of the stick. "Baby's skull," he said. His stick was lodged in the empty eye socket. "Infant flesh is a delicacy to these brutes."

"Not one of ours," Braga said. She pointed a finger at the shit-streaked skull. "That's the skull of a Wulfang baby. See the blunted snout?"

"One less Wulfang to worry about in the years to come," said Taboor. "Still, to eat a baby is…" He shook his head to show that his disgust was beyond words.

Sek dropped the stick and skull and stood. "I believe he's heading for Hag Mountain. He dropped this pile not long ago. We're very close."

"If we don't catch him before he reaches the Hag, then he's gone," Taboor said.

"He wants me to catch him," she told the men.

"How would you know that?" Taboor wanted to know.

"I know," she said with cold certainty. "I'll follow him into the mists if I have to."

"Do and be damned," Taboor rumbled.

"I'm already damned," she said, though her companions had no idea why she should say it.

"You go into those mists, you won't come out," Taboor argued. "Or you'll come out as a shadow of what you are now."

"You don't know what I am," she snapped. "If those mind-robbing mists take me from this shit-stinking world, so be it."

"Gods, but you're in a mood," he said, daring her anger.

"You're right, old friend," she said with a feral smile. "A killing mood." She stared at the mist-shrouded mountain in the distance. Twenty rods of shadowy woodland stood between them and Hag Mountain. The trees ahead offered plenty of opportunities for the Neph to ambush them. But it would also furnish cover for her war party's advance. "I'm riding alone into the woods," she told them. "You follow well behind and out of sight so if Nathor shows himself we'll spring a trap of our own."

"He could smash you before we have time to get to you," said Taboor.

"Nathor doesn't want to smash me," she said. "He has something else in mind."

Taboor exchanged dubious glances with Mulki and Sek. "I wish I knew what you're talking about, Braga."

"You know what to do. That is enough." She dug her heels into her mount and rode into the dark trees.

"Gods protect you," said Taboor.

She followed the little-used path through the woods, moving her mount at a slow, steady pace. She didn't concern herself with following Nathor's tracks now; she knew the giant was making it as easy as possible for her to catch up to him, and that this little trail would deliver her to him.

She recalled the few times she had crossed paths with him and understood now why the ugly creature had always retreated as if afraid. He'd been biding his time, waiting for her to reach what he considered optimal ripeness and readiness for bearing his ungodly offspring. Now that she knew he was her father, she understood why she had so often felt as if someone had been watching her from shadows. No doubt Nathor had relished watching her grow to womanhood. He must have seen her prove herself in battle against the

Wulfangs and go on to become leader of her tribe's warriors.

And now he judged that she was big-boned and strong enough to carry his little monster in her belly.

As she rode deeper into the snow-kissed trees, she pondered what it meant to be the descendent of a rogue angel and wondered why she had not been cursed with the gigantic stature and ugliness common to the Nephs. She was far from ugly. Everyone said she was beautiful, and more than a few men had tried to steal her maidenhead—much to their painful regret. She had yet to meet the man she couldn't best in a brawl. Somehow, she thought, I've inherited the strength of the Nephs but none of their physical traits—except that I'm taller and stronger than most men.

She suddenly felt eyes upon her and stiffened her spine. She scanned the trees and underbrush, but saw no one. She rode on, keeping her eyes sharp as blades. The closer she got to mist-wrapped Hag Mountain, the more deformed the trees became; their trunks were unnaturally twisted, their dead limbs bent into nightmarish shapes so that they resembled goblins from the underworld. Exposed roots had half-sprung from the ground as if the trees wanted to escape the cursed earth.

Now all the trees in front of her were dead, bewitched by some unnamed blight that spilled out from the mountain and poisoned the surrounding ground and everything growing on it. She could see the mysterious mountain clearly from here—closer than she'd ever before been to the dark, rocky crags and enveloping mists that perpetually cloaked its upper reaches. The mountain many feared and called Hag Mount, or simply the Hag.

It was said that certain sorcerers knew how to use the mountain's summit as a jump-off to other worlds. Braga had never believed this to be so, though her mother had always been a fierce believer. But now, as she gazed up at the towering colossus of barren rock, Braga found it wasn't hard to imagine that the Hag might be a lofty gateway to mysterious realms.

When her gaze drifted down from the high mist, she saw three giants standing like gnarled trees before her. Her battle-tested horse nickered, turning skittish in the unaccustomed presence of Nephs.

She bent forward to whisper calming words into the animal's left ear.

Nathor came forward and said in a high-pitched—almost womanly—voice : "You're slow, Little One. I thought you would get here much sooner." Then he laughed, and his laugh was also shrilly feminine.

The two giants standing with him laughed along, though there was nothing resembling amusement in their hideous faces. They all wore garments of thick brown fur, but no armor of any kind. They probably thought they didn't need armor against mere humans. Their tough-skinned muscular bulk was their armor.

Braga reached over her shoulder and unsheathed her sword. "Slow will be the manner of your death, you ugly pile of dung," she replied.

Again the three giants laughed, this time with genuine amusement in eyes that looked out from below jutting foreheads of lumpy bone. Great dagger-like teeth flashed within their gaping mouths. Teeth these beasts used when they devoured human flesh or the flesh of subhuman wolf-worshiping Wulfangs.

Braga's rage over what Nathor had done to her mother overrode her sudden fear that she and her small band could not best *three* Nephs in battle. Her hunger for vengeance overflowed her bosom and ran like a cold watercourse current down her arm, through her hand and into the blade of her sword. When she heard the pounding hooves of her warriors' horses coming up behind her, she loosed her eerie war cry and charged at Nathor, her blood up and her battle fury changing over to unbridled frenzy. Accelerating quickly into a hard gallop, her mount did not falter in the face of the three gargantuan trolls.

No longer laughing, Nathor stepped forward, raised his huge fist and brought it down upon her charging horse's head in what she knew was a killing blow. The brave animal immediately collapsed under her and skidded on splayed legs over rocky ground. Braga sprang from the dead horse's back, hit the ground with her blade extended over her head so that it didn't taste her own blood, and then rolled to her feet with the sword still in her determined grasp.

Riding hard between Sek and Taboor, Mulki unleashed his first arrow. It struck Nathor's thick chest dead center, but its shallowly embedded blade had no visible effect on the giant, who stomped, growling, toward Braga.

She gripped the pommel of her sword with both hands and swung it at Nathor's leg. It sliced a bloody runnel in the side of his muscular calf but did not slow his advance. He reached down for her just as another of Mulki's arrows stabbed into his stumpy forearm, making his hand miss her neck by a finger's length. She struck again with her blade, this time slashing a gash in his keg-size thigh. He bellowed like an angry woman, the high-pitched sound eerily incongruous with his physical aspect.

The giant on Nathor's left hurled a huge rock that knocked Mulki and his horse to the ground, while the one on Nathor's right charged forward to meet Taboor, who now had his bludgeon raised in his fist and was spurring his mount forward into the mêlée.

Braga saw what happened out of the corner of her eye, saw the giant knock Taboor from his horse with a great war-club, but she knew she had to focus her attention on her blooded foe Nathor and let Taboor take care of himself—if he still lived. Again she chopped with her blade, this time striking bone just below Nathor's knobby knee and causing him to list a little to his left.

Sek suddenly was beside her, lunging upward from his horse's back and driving his long spear into Nathor's soft belly. The giant grunted as he swatted Sek off his mount and hard onto the ground.

Braga cocked her sword over her shoulder, determined to chop Nathor to the ground so she could have off his big head, but before she could deliver another blow, the giant kicked out with his uninjured leg, his hairy foot and hooked toes striking her chest. She flew backward, losing her grip on the sword. She landed on her back, and her head bounced on the hard earth, knocking her helm off and freeing her war-braids. Darkness momentarily removed her from the fray. When she opened her eyes, she was looking up at the mist-cloaked mountain and wondered if she were dreaming of this haunted place. Then a smaller mountain blocked her view—the mountainous Nathor, looking down at her with his hideous grin. He plucked Mulki's arrows from his chest and arm with hardly a wince. A small trickle of blood ran from the spear-wound in his belly.

"You stung me with your blade, Little One," Nathor said. "Now I'll give you a taste of my stinger." He began to untie the hemp holding up his fur breeches.

She rolled her head to the left to see what had become of her companions. She saw one of the giants pick up Mulki, bury its long teeth in Mulki's throat and bite off his head, blood splattering a dead tree. She couldn't see Sek or Taboor but she heard the awful sounds of teeth rending soft flesh and bone, and she reckoned they too were dead—or were being eaten alive. She tried to get up, but Nathor planted a foot on her chest to hold her easily in place while he freed his stinger.

Braga looked up at the strange root jutting from between his legs and was overcome with revulsion. At the end of the foot-long vein-ridged shaft were two hideous heads! Though still a virgin, Braga had seen stiff wands of a few lustful men before, but never one with twin heads. If he managed to get that monstrous prick inside her, her innards could be permanently mangled. How could Nathor possibly believe she could bear his offspring? She surmised that his brain took up very little space in that huge skull of his.

She tried to wrest his massive foot off her chest, but she couldn't budge it. His talon-like toenails pricked her chin. His heel prevented her from drawing the dagger she wore on her hip. "You'll kill me with that thing," she shouted up at him.

He laughed, flashing a mouthful of long yellow teeth. "No, Little One, my two-headed beast will not kill you," he said in his grating high-pitched voice. "It will make you stronger."

She looked into his darkly shining eyes and vowed, "If you put a baby in me I'll cut it out before I birth it."

"Not if I chain you," Nathor crooned. "And chain you I will."

Trying not to listen to the horrible crunching of her dead companions' bones as the other Nephs devoured their remains, Braga shouted: "Then I'll strangle myself with your chains!"

He laughed again, then abruptly stopped laughing, a grave expression settling into his revolting face. "My kind is dying off," he said. "Women of your race can no longer bear our offspring. The bitches die before three cycles of the moon. But you are not like them. You sprang from my own seed and will be sturdy enough to bear my spawn. You will become legendary as the savior of Nephs. You should be honored, daughter."

She hawked up a wad of spit and propelled it at his foot. "There's your honor."

Nathor made a clicking noise in the back of his throat.

"And you are not my father," she told him. "Your cursed race *should* die out."

"And you with it? We have the same blood. Did your mother not confess the truth of it? I see in your eyes that she did. Your lips may lie but your eyes speak true. You *know* I fathered you."

He suddenly lifted his foot off her chest and said, "And now you will receive my seed and become the mother of your sibling."

Before she had a chance to spring to her feet and flee, Nathor bent down, ripped off her breeches, wrenched open her legs, fell to his knees and battered the tender lips of her sex with his two-headed prick. He effortlessly pinned her arms to the ground. She squirmed and tried to move her hips to foil his aim, but it was no use. He was too strong. He was going to stick his grotesque tool inside her and there was nothing she could do to stop him. Tears of outrage welled in her eyes, and she gritted her teeth to keep from screaming.

"Stop! In the name of God I command you to cease this depravity!" A man's voice. Booming with righteous wrath. "Unman that woman, foul fiend!"

Nathor froze, then looked back over his shoulder. Braga followed his gaze to see a man in a monk's robe *walking on the mist* at the base of Hag Mountain. His face was masked by darkness within the cowl he wore over his head. He held before him a staff as tall as he, but it was no ordinary staff—it was the sign of the Cross Cult savior's crucifixion. And as Braga and the Nephs looked on, the cross burst into bright white flames, seemingly without burning the hand that held it.

Nathor stood up and backed away from the air-floating holy man. The other two Nephs were already fleeing into the dusk.

"Be gone, fiend!" shouted the sorcerer, brandishing the flaming cross as if it were a weapon. And perhaps, it was.

With a high-pitched wail, Nathor pulled up his breeches, turned on his chunky heels and ran off.

Braga got to her feet, picked up her own breeches, stepped into them and snugged them on her hips.

The sorcerer came forward, stepped down from the mist and onto the ground. The fiery cross suddenly flamed out. The wooded staff was not a bit charred. The fire hadn't touched it.

"Thank you, Mist Walker," said Braga.

"My honor," he said, pushing back his cowl to reveal the face of an ordinary man with flowing locks of startling white. His face was not the face of an old man; his countenance did not tally with the white of his hair. Braga wondered if something otherworldly had robbed his hair of color.

"I am Thomas," he said, his voice a pleasant burr. His strange accent gave his words an odd thickness as they rolled off the back of his tongue.

She nodded. "I am Braga." She looked for the first time at the grisly remains of her fallen companions. "Those were my warriors. Good men, and dear to my people."

"Such senseless slaughter," said Thomas. "Are you injured?"

She shook her head. Nathor's foot had left a deep ache behind her bosom, but she did not think any bones were broken. She glanced at her helm, which had been crushed flat by the foot of a fleeing giant. As she bent down to retrieve her sword, she was overcome with dizziness and would have fallen had not the sorcerer caught her in his arms.

"Sit," he said as he eased her down.

She settled her rump on the earth, bent her legs, bridged her arms across her knees and rested her head on her arms. She closed her eyes and felt the world turning as if trying to spin her off it. A steady roaring in her ears held the echo of Nathor's womanish wailing. Even with eyes closed she could still see the mutilated remains of Taboor, Sek and Mulki, and the images sickened her. Her weakness infuriated her. She wanted to jump up and run until the moment of frailty passed, but her swimming head held her in place and the world went on trying to spin her into the sky.

Something touched her shoulder. She lifted her head and saw Thomas offering the bladder of water he'd found on her dead horse.

"Drink," he said.

She drank, then put her head back down and drifted into a red darkness between sleep and wakefulness. When she looked up some time later, the sorcerer had a campfire burning and was roasting a rabbit on a makeshift spit. "How did you catch it?" she asked.

"The Lord provides," he said, a tight smile on his lips.

"I didn't know a Cross Cult man could be a sorcerer," she said. Though the man had saved her from impalement on Nathor's two-headed prick, she didn't entirely trust this Mist Walker.

Thomas chuckled. "I wasn't always thus," he said. "One doesn't go into the mists of that mountain without being changed in some manner. It's a matter of survival."

"You went willingly?" Her natural curiosity often led her to make imprudent inquiries. She sensed she was making one now.

He shook his head, gazed a long moment into the flames of the campfire, and then said, "The story of how I ended up on that mountain would be long in the telling."

She shrugged. "This has the feel of a long night, does it not?"

"It does, at that," he said. "The rabbit's almost done. After we eat, I'll tell you of my extraordinary journey and subsequent adventures. Campfires have a way of drawing tales out of one."

She noticed that he had disposed of the bloody remnants of the deadly carnage; she was grateful that she no longer had to look at the pitiful remains of her once-great warriors. Soon he cut her a generous portion of the roasted meat and gave her a cup of dark wine. They ate in silence. The small game was tasty and the wine was satisfyingly tart and not too dry. After they had supped, Braga belched heartily to show her appreciation for the repast.

Then the Mist Walker told his tale.

V. THE MONK'S TALE

I was an insignificant monk in my third year at a monastery in a world beyond this mystical mountain when the visions started. As a boy I'd been cursed with too much imagination, so when the visions first presented themselves to me I mistakenly assumed I was finally imagining myself into madness. I spent most days in the scriptorium, illuminating manuscripts with fantastical illustrations, so naturally I suspected that my fanciful artwork had somehow corrupted my view of the mundane world. But my visions became too painful to dismiss as mere art-crazed whimsy. They were always accompanied by fierce pains in my head, as if some invisible beast were digging its claws into my skull. Then a bright white light would appear before my eyes—or perhaps *inside* my eyes. The pain would drive me to my knees, from which position I desperately prayed for the Lord to spare me further excruciation. The Lord, it seemed, had other plans for me.

From that pulsing white light it always came on shimmering wings, its face too fierce to look upon, and yet I could not tear my eyes from it. It filled the whole sky at first, but the closer it came, the smaller it became—a celestial paradox that confounded my mental capacities. I knew I was seeing an angel, and from its furious aspect I thought it must be an Avenging Angel sent to exact God's wrath upon the vilest of low of sinners. The angel wielded a weapon too terrible to have been forged by man—a fiery sword powerful enough to lay waste an entire army with a single stroke.

When I looked into the angel's shinning eyes, I read the creature's unholy intent. This angel had not come on the Lord's business; it had come of its own misguided volition, no longer under the auspices of Heaven. It had come to vent its rage upon humanity, to deal indiscriminate slaughter. A masterless angel bent on wanton mayhem.

But why had *I* been chosen to see this coming calamity? What was I, a monk of lowest rank, to do with this prophetic knowledge? My superiors at the monastery were at a loss, knowing no way to help me, nor what to make of my visions. In fact, most of the brothers came to regard me as mad, and a few even thought I was possessed of devils. You see, my visions invariably set me to screaming, and each time they ended, they left me blubbering and babbling like a madman. I suppose I *was* mad. But I was convinced of the truth of what I had seen. A great evil was coming from the unlikeliest place. A renegade angel, having deserted Heaven, was coming to unleash its inexplicable wrath upon mankind.

But that wasn't the worst of what I divined. This rogue angel's actions were all but certain to spark a war between Heaven and Hell. Mankind would be caught in the middle of this Great War, and the fate of humanity would hang in precarious balance. Lucifer was going to mobilize his dark armies and join the fray. Spurred on by the renegade angel, Lucifer and his fallen angels would storm the Heavenly Gates and attempt to bring about the fall of Heaven.

This terrible knowledge was more than I could bear. I attempted to kill myself with a kitchen knife, but Brother William stopped me before the blade cut too deeply into my throat. They bound me with rope and sat with me, praying tirelessly, until the crisis passed.

Several days later a new vision came to me: a mist-ravened mountain, its steep craggy walls inhospitable to human habitation or visitation. Nevertheless, I instantly understood I had to find that mountain and challenge its elevations. I sketched the mountain and showed it around the monastery, in the hope that the mountain's uniquely forbidding outcroppings and scarcity of vegetation would make it recognizable to at least one of the other monks. Brother Alenard studied my drawing, making the peculiar humming sounds he always made when puzzling out a problem, and then he suddenly tapped it with his finger and said, "I know this singular mountain. It's on the edge of the Carpathian range."

Two days later I departed the monastery and set out for the Carpathian Mountains with a crude map Brother Alenard had sketched for me. Despite inclement weather and the usual hardships of foot-travel, I made my destination some long days later. Indeed, it *was* the mountain of my vision—of that there could be no mistake. I spent the night in prayerful meditation at the foot of the forlorn mount, and began my ascent at dawn. I climbed a narrow rocky trail along jagged cliffs and dangerous precipices, driven by earthly instinct and by the belief that the Lord was guiding me on my outlandish pilgrimage. My ascent took me into layers of mists such as I had never seen. The high altitudes and the seductive mists effected changes in my perceptions. The ground beneath me disappeared. I found myself walking a truly visionary road. My feet found support upon low clouds and thick mists. Faith made me unafraid. I was treading upon the very hand of God. Certainly my fate was in His hands. Nightfall did not slow my ascent; the mists glowed with otherworldly light. Up and up I went, until fear caught up with me and I was all at once terrified of being swallowed up by the strangely illuminated mist. Then I was falling through failing clouds, falling through a hole in the world, falling, surely, to my death. I don't know what happened next. Darkness took me before I hit any sort of bottom, and I woke up on top of this mountain you now see behind me.

A single tree grows from its otherwise barren summit. The Blood Tree. Perhaps you have heard of it? It is mythologized in some quarters. Oddly enough, I saw myself cutting a small gash in its soft bark and then placing my mouth to the wound to drink of its blood-sap. The mystical properties of that tree's blood are legendary, I now know, and drinking that crimson sap infused me with secret knowledge few men have ever possessed.

Thereupon, I was beset with a blizzard of luminous visions, each one grounded in truth, each one more fantastical than the last. I was swimming through a stream of lost souls, some of them quite hostile to the living, but I managed to stay afloat, to stave off the hostiles and assimilate what was shown to me. When at last the mist cleared a little, I met myself on that mountaintop—and I mean that quite literally. I became my own tutor. I had much to learn and even more to teach, for my knowledge was vast and apocryphal. I had lived many lives in many worlds, and the prospect of more lives loomed—subject, it now seems, to how impending events in your world play out.

You see—or you will soon enough—I met *you* on Hag Mountain, too. I had a vision of our meeting and of your futurity, of terrible events that will soon transpire in your world and of the part you are destined to play in them. And that, fair Braga, is why I am here.

I am come to tutor you so that you will be ready to face the brutal angel Rahab and to steal his harrowing sword.

VI. BLOODY TIDINGS

Braga gave the man a fierce look. She fought the impulse to thrash him where he sat. She clenched her hands together to keep them from the mad monk's throat. She considered how best to attack this man's absurd claims and expose him as the soothsaying trickster he almost certainly was. Finally, she showed her teeth in a glee-less grin and said, "I think you *are* mad, Mist Walker. How can a Cross Cult man be a sorcerer? I've been given to understand that your one god and his living-dead savior son forbid their followers to truck with elementals and lesser gods."

"Aye, so the Christian Church teaches. Everything is a matter of interpretation. What I learned on that mountain gave *me* to know I can never be part of any religious group corrupted by greed and run by men hungry to steal God's glory. I know, too, that the art of sorcery is not inimical to the belief in the Father, the Son and the Holy Ghost. Sorcery is a tool, just as your sword is a tool, an implement of war, protection and power. You may use your weapon for good or ill. It is the same with the mystic arts. A sorcerer pure of heart may serve the Lord and dedicate his personal powers to Heaven."

"You talk a good game," she said, "but I think you are full of holy dung. I've never been on Hag Mountain. You cannot know my future."

"There are many futures. Not just the one. It is left to you to choose your path and make your destiny. It is my destiny to help you make your choice."

"Namely, to steal this raging angel's sword." She couldn't help but grin as she said this. "Gods, but you're an amusing fool!"

Thomas returned her grin. Then he said, "I will take you to the Blood Tree and you will drink its sap. Then you will have a clearer vision of your place in this worldly drama, and you will know my words are true."

She shook her head. "My destiny is not on that mountain," she told him. "I am going after the giant who slaughtered my friends and killed my mother. If I am destined for anything, it's ending that walking dung-heap's miserable life."

"How shortsighted you are! There are larger issues at stake. Don't you see that? Considerations of greater import than your low lust for vengeance. You have an awesome responsibility to—"

"Enough!" She jumped to her feet and glared at him over the campfire's waning flames. "I may be shortsighted but the reach of my blade is long. I have no time for your fairy-tales. I'm going to find one of the runaway horses and go after those murdering giants."

A strange look came into the man's face. The whites of his eyes eclipsed his pupils and he began to tremble within his monk's habit. Braga thought the man must be sinking into a fit of madness, but then his blue eyes reappeared, quivering within deepened sockets, and he said, "Rahab has come. He begins his slaughter with the Nephalim." Then his face returned to its accustomed countenance, and he shrugged. "Not that you could've dispatched those brutes yourself, had you caught them. Unless you possessed Angel Steel. When that weapon is yours, no foe will be unconquerable."

She roughly seized his robe. "Your visions tell you this? Nathor is dead?"

"It is so," said Thomas, a weary expression on his face. "Don't you see? Your unnatural heritage makes you capable of wielding the harrowing blade. No ordinary human could touch it without dying. You have angel-sweetened blood in your veins. Those rebellious angels who first mated with mortal women bequeathed their Heavenly seed to the subsequent hybrid race of monsters. But the corrupted angel strain of blood was diluted enough by the time of your conception that your mother didn't give birth to a monster. You are unique in all the worlds. You are the only mortal fit to wield Angel Steel. Call it destiny, or call it an accident of Heaven. Whatever you call it, you cannot deny the truth of it."

"And all I have to do is steal this magical weapon from a wrathful angel," she mocked him. "Do your visions tell you how I can do that without losing my head?"

"You won't do it without my help. All I know for certain is that you have to steal it during the time of the black sun."

"The black sun?"

"When this planet's shadow falls on the face of the sun and darkens day to dusk. That will happen two days from now. And that is when you must strike the renegade angel a crippling blow with his own sword."

Braga heard the sudden sound of hoofbeats in the near distance. She grabbed her sword and turned toward the sound of the approaching rider, ready to meet any possible danger.

Thomas groaned, then said, "Bad tidings, I'm afraid. The worst you can imagine."

"Quiet!" she said through clenched teeth.

Gragor rode out of the dead trees and reined his hard-ridden mount to a halt before the fire. Braga caught him as he slid off the horse's back. "Dead," he said in a hoarse whisper. "They're all dead."

She eased him to the ground. His head had been bloodied and there was a long gash across his chest. "Who's dead?" she asked him, unable to keep her voice as gentle as she had intended.

"Wulfangs killed everyone in the village and put it to torch. They must've left me for dead. I woke up and everyone was slaughtered. We couldn't stop them. I'm sorry…"

"*Everyone?*" she said, scarcely able to believe Gragor's words, yet knowing they were true.

Gragor nodded. A trickle of blood caught in his eyelash. "They surprised us," he recounted. "There were too many of them. We fought hard but they would not be bested. They must've enlisted their tribes from the east. There were easily two hundred Wulfang warriors. I'm sorry, Braga. I should've died fighting them."

"No. You were meant to live. To bear witness to what you saw."

Gragor shook his head, sending another bloody trickle from his head wound. "It shames me to live." Now tears joined the blood trails on his cheeks.

Braga slapped his jaw. "Remember who you are," she told him. "Remember what you saw, but don't lament your part in it. You are blameless. The Wulfangs are the culprits, and they will pay. You and I will make them howl in despair."

Looking down, he nodded miserable assent.

Braga scooped up a handful of white from a patch of melting snow and cleaned his wounds with it. Thomas watched in silence, his face grim.

"Tyka…" she said, her voice catching in the back of her throat.

A look of loathing came into Gragor's face. "A Wulfang blade halved her little skull."

"Then her death was quick. She probably never felt it." She stood and turned to the sorcerer. "You knew of this before I did."

"It came to me with the hoof-beats of your man's horse," said Thomas. "I saw images of the slaughter only moments before you learned of it."

"Knowledge is useless when it comes too late, eh, sorcerer?"

"There are limits to all worldly things," he said with a slight bow of his head.

She stood before him and put her hand on his shoulder. "Now tell me," she said. "What must I do to get this Angel Steel?"

VII. INTO THE HAG

Though raised from early childhood to be fearless in dangerous endeavors, Braga recognizes that the giddy tingling in her chest and the tightness in her neck are her body's reactions to fear. The fear found her the moment she stepped onto Hag Mountain, and it is growing now that they have entered thick mist. Thomas the monk leads them and lights the way with his staff held aloft, the wooden cross glowing with phantom flames that give no heat, nor burn the hand holding it. Gragor walks behind Thomas, and Braga walks behind him so that she might catch him if he falters from his wounds or prod him if he wavers from fear. And the mist-enveloped Hag *is* a fear-making place. Every farfetched tale she has ever heard of this mountain now seems perfectly plausible, every tale's fabled horror perfectly conceivable.

As the rocky path along the edge of a steep cliff takes them into higher elevations and into ever-thickening fog, Braga wonders how far she can trust the sorcerer. Has he truly come into her world to guide her and assist her in her fight against evil enemies, or has he come to use her for his own secret purposes? Surely there is much the man has not told her. She wonders how forthcoming he would be if she put the point of her sword to his throat and demanded a full confession of his sorcerous secrets.

"Mist Walker," she calls to him. "How long were you on this mountain before you came down to meet me?"

Without breaking his practiced stride and without looking back, he says, "Time on this mountain's summit does not flow as it does in worldly realms. Perhaps you feel it already. The closer we get to the top, the further outside of time we will be."

"What's he talking about?" Gragor whispers over his shoulder to Braga.

"Time, young man," answers Thomas, demonstrating an acute sense of hearing. "Time is lost to the mists of this mount. This is an eternal place. Eternity resides in each non-moment. Or to put it another way: This mountain offers respite from the cycle of life and death. On Hag's summit you are neither alive nor dead. Time does not touch you. There you are suspended between mortality and immortality."

"And if I drive my sword through your heart you would not die?" she scoffs.

Thomas laughs. "When we reach the summit, you may test it. I will feel a slight tickle, no more. No blood, no physical damage."

"I don't believe it," says Gragor.

"Mayhap I'll take you up on that tempting offer," says Braga.

"As you wish. But I should warn you, there are creatures we are likely to encounter near the summit that you will need to dispatch with your blade. Some say they are the Hag's guardians. Perhaps they are, but I rather believe they are...what's the word? Anomalies. Forms of life too deficient to survive in other worlds. Accidental creatures. Or perhaps they are the nightmare spawn of dreamers in other worlds. While it may be amusing to speculate on their origins, you must never forget that the Izards are extremely dangerous and will have out your heart in the blink of an eye if you let them get too close."

"Izards? What manner of beasts are they?" Braga wants to know.

"That's my name for them. I believe you have lizards in your world. They resemble lizards, though they are nearly as big as hogs.

They scuttle over rocks and crags rather quickly, and yet they move awkwardly because their tails are so long and thick. Though they have three eyes, they seem to have poor eyesight, which means they won't see you until you stumble upon them. The point is, don't stumble. Move with stealth."

"I can hardly move at all in this fog," Gragor grumbles. "How can I avoid your bloody Izards?"

"Stay close to me and the light. Izards are not like the Nephalim. They are too dumb to fear the cross and all it symbolizes, but the bright light hurts their eyes."

"Can't bloody blame the buggers. If I had three eyes I wouldn't like the light either," says Gragor. Braga is glad to see that he is regaining his mocking humor. He is moving with more agility, using Sek's spear as a staff.

"Now we must be silent so we can hear the dry scuttle of the Izards before we come upon them."

"But I would know more of this Lucifer you mentioned," Braga says. "I think my mother spoke of him as some sort of demon."

"The fallen angel Lucifer reigns in Hell. We will speak more of him at another time. For now, be silent."

They move on in silence. They follow the cliff-edge trail to its end, and then skirt insurmountable outcroppings and climb a treacherous incline of loose rocks and rough sand to a higher footpath. Braga is beginning to understand what the monk meant about the passage of time on this mountain; it seems that they have been climbing for days—as though her life before stepping onto the Hag was but a dream. Yet she is not tired. She wonders if she is somehow drawing energy from the mountain. The mist is so thick she can taste it on her tongue and feel it accumulating in her nose, down the back of her throat and in her chest. It is cool, almost soothing, and she thinks it's starting to make her light-headed, as if she'd drunk too much tavern ale.

Gragor abruptly halts in front of her and stares at the wall of rock on his left.

"What is it?" she asks, stopping beside him.

"Faces," he answers, childlike wonder in his voice. "In the rock.

Don't you see them?"

She follows his fixed gaze but sees nothing, save raw-edged rock in the dim glow from the sorcerer's bright cross, its eerie light filtering back to them through the unnatural fog. "I see no faces," she says. "Mist Walker, bring your light."

The monk glides back to join them, a look of displeasure on his face. He holds the cross of heatless fire close to the rock face and widens his eyes.

"I saw them," insists Gragor. "They were there. And they were... whispering."

"It's the mist," Braga says, "making you see things that aren't there."

Gragor raises his spear and touches it to the dark granite. "This was a woman's mouth. See this dark spot? And these, her eyes. I swear it."

"And what did she say?" Braga asks. "Did she ask you for a kiss?"

"No!" His face blushes crimson in the white light. "I think they were...I don't know. But it seemed...important."

The monk says, "You saw the faces of those who lost their souls to this mountain. Some of them died here on the Hag, others went back down to wander the world as soulless beings, waiting for death to end their misery."

"We could lose our souls?" Gragor steps away from the wall of granite. Braga grabs his arm to keep him from falling backward to his death.

The monk suddenly looks very grave. "We are always in danger of losing our souls, young man," he says. "Your main purpose in life is to make it out of this world with your soul intact. The reason we are here now is to mount a defense against those powerful forces that would steal the soul of the world."

"I don't understand," Gragor says.

"I know, lad. And that's all right. For now, just put your faith in Braga and me, and keep your eyes sharp for those Izards. Come now, we are near the summit and time is already stretched to the breaking-point."

"I'm not sure I trust you myself, sorcerer," Braga tells him. "Your words have the ring of madness, and yet they feel true."

He smiles. "Once you've had your drink from the Blood Tree, all will be clear to you."

He turns and resumes in his surefooted trek up the mountain. Gragor and Braga warily follow him through the mist illumined by his magic cross.

A short or a long time later (it is impossible to know which), they cross paths with an Izard. It seems to come out of the mountain rock itself, scuttling noisily, its overlarge tail twitching clumsily and its three big eyes reflecting the white light of the cross. Its great mouth gapes, showing teeth nearly as long as tusks. Gragor gives a startled yell, but he reacts with admirable reflex and drives the wide blade of his spear into the creature's throat.

Braga draws her sword and swings it with both hands, its slightly curved blade hacking deep into the pebbled flesh at the base of the Izard's elongated skull. The beast screams and snaps its jaws, fat tail flailing. Gragor puts his weight behind his spear and pushes it deeper into the Izard's throat. Braga delivers a second chopping blow, nearly decapitating the creature. Its bestial screaming becomes a wet, gurgling wheeze. The porcine lizard falls silent, and stops thrashing its tail. Its three eyes turn milky in death. Its dark blood emits a foul odor, making Gragor cough and gag.

"Well done," the sorcerer says. "You not only slew the beast, but you also found a short-cut to the summit." Before they can ask what he means, he points a finger at the opening in the rock through which the Izard launched its ill-fated attack. "There."

"We're to crawl into that hole?" Gragor asks as he works his spear out the dead beast's throat.

"Yes."

"But if we meet another one of those things in there, we won't have room to wield our weapons. I don't fancy ending up in the belly of one of those buggers."

"We'll be fine. A short way in, the tunnel will open up to an inner hollow. You'll see."

Gragor grumbles a little, but he crouches down and follows the monk into the mouth of the tunnel. Braga goes in after them. They have to walk bent over because there isn't room to walk erect. The damp walls of the tunnel reflect the ghostly glow of the monk's cross. Braga imagines that they're moving through the throat of a leviathan, a gigantic monster her mother had once told her about. She damps down her imagination as they go deeper into the mountain. The monk was right: the tunnel leads to a vast cave-like space within the mountain.

The three of them can now walk upright. Gragor asks, "Who hollowed this out? And don't tell me fairytales of gnomes."

"I don't know. One legend tells of beings visiting from another star, but it doesn't suggest why they would've done this massive excavation."

"I thought you knew every bloody thing," Braga goads him.

The monk smiles. "No, there is much I don't know, and as you will see, the more you learn, the more questions you will have. That seems to be the way it always is with secret knowledge—or what you call sorcery. Now be on your guard. There may be other dangers lurking about."

"It's good to be out of that damned mist," Gragor observes as they follow an excavated path of stone along the curving wall of the cave. "At least we can see what comes at us next."

Braga glances over her shoulder to see three Izards clinging to the wall on the other side of the cavern. "We're being followed," she warns her companions. "But I think they are too slow to catch us."

"They may smell us but they can't see that far," says the monk. Then he raises the fiery cross higher, points with a long slender finger of his free hand and says, "There's the passage to the summit."

VIII. FALLEN GIANTS

Rahab surveyed the snowy field of slaughter and reveled in the carnage. The descendants of lustful *Mal'akh* lay in charred pieces upon the half-frozen ground, victims of his devastating sword. He had cut them down and dismembered their unsightly bodies with detached ease. Not until the three Nephalim were dead did Rahab pause to savor his bloody handiwork.

He picked up the decapitated head of one of the fallen giants by its ropey hair and addressed it in his sonorous voice: "So you escaped the great flood, cousin. Did you think you could hide your ugly bulk from Heaven's eyes? You had not the brain to match your mass. I did you a service by ending your miserable existence in this out-of-the-way world. You were never meant to be, conceived without the Father's blessing and cursed from birth. Tell me: How did you summon the will to survive? How did you refrain from ending your own pitiful life when you realized what you were?"

Rahab touched a white finger to the giant's lumpy forehead. "Speak."

The bodiless head blinked its remaining eye. Its thick, misshapen lips quivered, then the mouth opened and it spoke with a raspy whisper: "Afraid...to...die..."

"Fear kept you alive."

The giant's face wrinkled and furrowed, the head looking as if it were trying to nod itself.

"You feared an afterlife?"

"Yes..."

Seeing terror in the dead giant's eye, Rahab laughed. "You needn't have worried. Lucifer would not have such as you in his domain. You have no soul. Nothing awaits you but eternal darkness."

An expression of relief settles into the giant's face. Then the head speaks, not in answer to any question but of its own dwindling volition: "I...have...a daughter...Braga..."

"Yes, I watched you with her," Rahab said. "She is not like you. She is more *Mal'akh* than Nephalim. Though she is mortal, she is certainly more than human. I did not know of the existence of her kind. Perhaps I should take her apart to see what lies at her core. As for you, you pitiless abomination, I commend you to oblivion."

Rahab crushed the head between his hands and then hurled the lumpy, dripping mass across the dark sky. Taking a final pleasurable look at the bloody patch of ground, he attuned his preternaturally acute senses to the dead giant's female offspring, acquired energy from distant suns in the night sky, and then began to translate himself to the summit of the hollow mountain toward which the woman climbed. The earth shrank beneath his feet, and he took to the firmament, bending and shrinking the space between him and the targeted mountain.

A lone Wulfang lurking nearby saw Rahab's transit as a soundless flash of lighting. The Wulfang made a sign against evil, for it was well known among his kind that lightning on a clear night was the worst of omens.

IX. THE BLOOD TREE

As they approach the mouth of the tunnel the monk identified as passage to the mountaintop, Braga hears the whispering of faraway voices. When she looks around to spot the whisperers, she sees people moving along the carved walkways encircling the walls of the great cavern. But they are not ordinary people; they are transparent apparitions. Hundreds of them, seemingly going in circles to nowhere.

"Who are they?" she asks the monk.

"Lost souls, either unable or unwilling to leave this place. I don't know what draws them here. Ignore them. If they know you can see them they may try to follow us."

"But they can't leave with us. Can they?"

"Some of the braver souls might, but we must not be encumbered by their needful company. Come. We have but a short way to go now."

They enter the last tunnel and trudge up the steep incline, the incandescent cross lighting their way. The whispering dies away behind them. Soon they are moving into the mist again, and the monk tells them they are nearing the summit.

"Good," says Gragor, "I don't like being stuck in a place where you can lose your soul to the fog. And this damned tunnel is too… bloody close."

The mist thickens, hazing the cool flames of the monk's cross with a ghostly halo. Then all at once the mouth of the dank tunnel opens and disgorges them onto a flat expanse of volcanic rock. Sensing danger, Braga instinctively touches the haft of the dagger on her belt. The monk turns to face her, his white hair blowing in a wind that somehow does not move the oppressive mist.

"Be on your guard," he says. "This place attracts evil energies."

Gragor holds up his spear and says, "Let them come. I'm feeling a little evil myself."

"Keep your boasting to yourself, lad," the monk advises. "Certain of these ungodly entities would take such words as an invitation to possess your soul."

"Where is it?" Braga demands. "The tree."

"See that red glow yonder? The Blood Tree stands there."

"Then let's get to it. And save your scary fairytales for children. I don't want to hear them." In truth, she thinks the monk believes his words of evil entities—and she doesn't much doubt them herself—but she is eager to see this magical tree and discover what it has to teach her. She doesn't wish to approach the tree with a fearful heart, for fear might very well taint her communion with it and adversely affect her fate.

The monk nods. Braga has the feeling that he has read her thoughts and understands the personal desires underlying her gruff words. He moves off toward the luminous red mist. She and Gragor follow closely, buffeted by howling winds that have no effect on the mist.

The black tree is a thick nest of limbs bent into or reaching for impossible angles. Some limbs are gnarled and knotted, others forked, and a few perfectly straight and true. The trunk is stumpy and looks as if unnatural forces shaped it into strange, twisting bends as it grew out of the barren rock beneath it. Something in the tree's overall appearance suggests that it erupted all at once from the earth. The tree is totally black, but it gives off a crimson glow that makes the surrounding mist appear bloody.

Though it isn't uncommonly tall, the tree seems to tower over them. Its ominous presence wrings a shudder out of Braga, and her hand moves to the sword sheathed on her back. She senses that the tree is trying to speak to her in some inaudible tongue, to impart something of vital importance. Gragor hangs well back, afraid to get too close to the tree. Thomas the monk stands beside Braga, holding his burning cross aloft.

The monk says, "It recognizes you."

Braga makes no response. She keeps her eyes locked upon the black tree.

"Some years ago a book crossed my desk at the monastery scriptorium. A tome of obscure origin, it bore the title *The Book of Tree*. It contained a drawing representative of this very tree, though of course that was before my initial visit to this mountain. The text was Sumerian, very difficult to translate, but I worked at it for days and finally coaxed a sensible translation from the foreign tongue into Latin. When in my excitement I showed it to my superior, he ordered me to burn the book and my translation and to forget the corrupting ideas to which I'd been exposed. Ever obedient, I tossed it and all my work on *Cruor Nemus* into the fire and prayed for help in forgetting what I'd read. But of course I *didn't* forget—couldn't forget. Even now I could quote passages for you."

"I didn't come to this place to hear more of your stories," Braga says with a sharp tongue.

"My point is this: The Blood Tree may in fact be the same tree of knowledge in the Christian cannon, in that its proffered knowledge carries a curse. There is always a price to be paid for forbidden knowledge. I say this to you as warning. It's not too late to leave this place without drinking of the tree's blood-sap. Destiny is a delicate thing. It may, in some cases, be altered."

"I will taste its blood," she says, again touching the haft of her dagger, "but first I will test the truth of your words."

She draws the dagger and plunges its blade deep into his belly.

His face registers surprise as he drops the cross and clutches at her offending hand.

X. THE MESSENGER

Melchizedek found Rahab at the temporal verges above the summit of the murky mountain.

"Prince of Light," Rahab greeted his estranged celestial brother.

"Have you come to dissuade me from my worldly course?"

"I am come by the will of the Father," Melchizedek answered. "Your intentions on the corporeal planes are counter to the will of Heaven."

Rahab laughed. "As you well know, I have divorced myself from the will of Heaven. I intend to make these earthly planes my own, to make them sing and yowl loud enough to be heard above and below. Loud enough to make Lord Lucifer envious."

"You know where such a course will lead. You must not be a force for chaos and mayhem."

"My Prince," Rahab mocked again, "you know Creation requires chaos."

"But you are not meant to be the instrument thereof. I beg you, desist. For our Father's sake."

"Save your begging for Him. Do not belittle yourself by begging me."

"Then this is our last meeting as brothers," Melchizedek said. "When next we meet, our swords will clash and you will be crippled and forever outcast, bereft of the love of your Father."

Rahab produced a beatific smile, and then reached into the feathered folds of his torso to seize the malleable handle of his secreted sword. "Nay, Prince," he said through the smile, "I am not now your brother." He freed the smoky sword from his person and swung the radiant blade at Melchizedek's head, but the Prince of Light parried the blow with the fiery sword which materialized at the end of his powerful right extremity.

The single clash of celestial blades filled the sky with blinding lightning. The resulting thunder shook the earth, setting off powerful tremors even below the planet's seas.

"You know I cannot fight you now, Rahab."

"Go then. Go groveling to the Father for permission to do battle. You know where to find me."

With a countenance of uncharacteristic anguish, Melchizedek held his magnificent sword aloft and jetted homeward.

Rahab disinterestedly watched the Archangel flash out the abstracted space of this realm, and then he returned his avid attentions to the mortals on the summit of the time-misted mountain.

XI. BLOOD RIDDLES

Slipping her dagger's blade into the monk's belly is a little like stabbing water thickened with mud—mushy and unsatisfying.

The blade comes out clean. Bloodless.

He says, "Now you see."

Braga nods. She sheaths the dagger. "I trusted your words," she says. "Had they been false, you would be dying. Now I know my trust was not misplaced."

"And I know lying to you could prove fatal," he says with a miniscule smile. Then he retrieves his glowing staff.

Gragor steps forward in the red haze. "And if you put the blade in my belly I won't be hurt?"

"That's right, lad," says the monk. "Here, we are not in any one world. We stand upon the threshold to many possible worlds. We are somewhere between the physical and the spiritual, neither mortal nor immortal."

"And you know all this because you once drank the sap from this tree," Braga reflects.

"Yes," he says with a sudden air of impatience. "Now use your dagger to puncture the bark and then put your mouth to the wound and drink."

"How much?"

"As much as you need. You will know when you've had enough."

"I'll know," she says, as if suddenly spellbound. Apprehensive, she stares at the black tree.

"The tree will tell you."

"Bloody talking tree and bodies that won't bleed," Gragor muses aloud. "I must be dreaming."

"In a sense, you *are* dreaming," says the sorcerer. "But dreaming with your whole being, not just part of your sleeping mind. And *this* dream is already come true."

Gragor shakes his head in confused wonder.

Braga draws her dagger and steps up to the black tree. "This won't…hurt it?"

"No. The Blood Tree is not sentient, though it possesses and dispenses sentience of a kind. And it has remarkable recuperative powers."

"You talk in riddles," she huffs.

She touches the tree's trunk with the fingertips of her free hand. The dark bark is rough like old skin, though its underlying softness suggests flesh—vibrant, yet cool to the touch. As she prepares to pierce it with the dagger, an intense flash of light blinds her and a deafening thunderclap sends her reeling to the ground. The Hag's summit shudders beneath her back.

"Bloody hell," Gragor groans from a supine position. "What was that?"

"The beginning of what we must try to stop," says the sorcerer. Somehow, he has managed to remain on his feet.

Braga's sight slowly returns as the afterimage of lightning fades from the backs of her eyes. Thomas is pointing a bony finger at the tree. He holds the crossed staff slightly askew, its heatless flames illuminating the surrounding red haze so that the entire scene is haloed in crimson and resembles a blurred painting done by an artist enraptured with religious fervor. "Quickly," he urges.

She crawls to the tree and plunges the dagger into its trunk. Up on her knees, she puts her mouth to the wound and begins to drink the dark red sap bleeding from the cut. At first it is tasteless, but after a few swallows she detects a salty sweetness with an unpleasant edge of fermentation, as if she were sucking the juice of rotting fruit from a sickly tree. A ringing fills her ears. The blood-sap burns her throat and kindles liquid fire in her belly, but she somehow knows it will not damage her innards. A powerful sense of well-being fills her and she is thirsty for more. She sucks harder, swallows faster. The ringing in her ears turns musical. The most beautiful music she has ever heard. Her body is the instrument, its every fiber yielding to the skilled fingers of an invisible musician and singing in divine harmony with a faraway ghostly chorus. She feels a warm, wet emptiness between her legs, an intense longing for something outside herself, a drunken lustful need for something to fill a fundamental void within.

Then the Blood Tree begins to sing.

She falls back on her haunches, blood-sap dripping from the corners of her mouth, music sounding from her pores in bright crystalline notes. She sees the music as diamonds floating on a sea of red and purple motes—the glowing specks from which empty space springs. The air takes on new depths, opening up mote-flecked corridors of sound and light that invite her deeper into yearning space and toward the infinite worlds waiting at the ends of those purple corridors. She must choose a path, single out a corridor to go into, lest she explode into chaotic directions and into the death and dissolution of her soul in eternal darkness.

Spinning on the axis of her physical form, she sees shifting corridors everywhere she looks, one channel blurring into another, the corridor walls composed of starry purple motes built upon smaller specks and those upon even smaller ones. Something—some indefinable force—is pulling her, pushing her, forcing her into a choice of direction. Then all at once she is moving backward, retracing the journey from home to Hag Mountain with blurring speed. She is home; the journey to the Hag never happened. She is but a formless spirit witnessing the slaughter of her people, unable to intervene. She sees a Wulfang blade halve Tyka's head. She hears the gut-wrenching screams of women and children as they fall under the Wulfangs' murderous weapons.

Next comes the shock of seeing herself in the thick of the fierce battle, wielding her sword against the swarming invaders. She chops them down, one after another, cutting her way through their ranks. A Wulfang warrior with a rusty helm and a bloodied snout attacks from behind and drives his blade into her back, severing her spine. She is dead the moment she hits the ground, her spirit instantaneously severed from its fallen husk. Facing her risen spirit-double, she says: *This never happened.* Her double communicates to her: *It did and it didn't. You are neither here nor there but both here and there. Alive and dead.*

She turns away, repulsed by still more maddening riddles. New corridors loom, opening in all directions, shuffling and reshuffling like fortuneteller's cards, fanning one into another. She flies down the yawning throat of one of the ethereal passageways. And she is back on the crimson summit of the Hag, facing the cross-bearing monk. "I don't understand," she whispers.

"Yes, you do," he insists. "Don't fight it."

Gragor's face floats before her. It is a face twisted by demonic torment. His black eyes are ablaze. His spear flies from his hand and lodges, quivering, in the black tree. Blood-sap drips from the wound.

Corridors shift, shuffle.

The dripping blood-sap reverses direction and runs up the trunk and back into the tree, and the spear flies back to Gragor's hand.

Transfixed, Braga stares at the flaming cross in the monk's hand. The ghostly flames are consuming the red haze, leaping hungrily, eating the world, devouring the corridors to all worlds, until only black nothingness remains.

And Braga is nowhere.

XII. ANGELIC ALCHEMY

A white face as big as the sky fills her tentative field of vision. Perceptions and dimensional perspectives defy confounded reason. Behind and below her, down a glittering purplish corridor, lies the Hag's hazed summit. Her erstwhile traveling companions are there beneath the blooded black tree, frozen in timelessness.

The colossal face speaks: "There you are."

"You are *mal'akh*," she says.

"I was. Now I am something for which you have no words, neither Watcher nor Messenger. I am called Rahab. But I see in your eyes you already know something of me. We are, after all, related. You know this as well."

Rahab's eyes are a shimmering black. She sees her own twinned reflections in them, two different aspects of what she is—or *may* be. She says, "I am Braga of Faery Valley, warrior of the Heathcoat Clan."

Rahab seems to come closer, shrinking as he does. The effect is disorienting and Braga takes a step backward, realizing then that she is standing upon viscous mist. *Mist Walker,* she thinks, amazed.

Now standing three heads taller than she, Rahab says, "Your clan was destroyed. You are a warrior without a clan. We are alike in that respect. The tilt-eyed men of the quaking island race have a word that comes closest to describing what I am. They call their feudal warriors *samurai,* but a *samurai* without a master is called *Ronin.* I once served God the Father, but now I serve no master."

"Why does your god not strike you down?" she asks.

"Perhaps the Father is curious to see what I will do, now that I have slipped His gilded leash. He does not like to destroy His favored creations."

"What truck have you with me?"

Rahab smiles. "We shall see. Though I believe you may already have something in mind."

"You know my mind?" She fears that he knows she intends to steal his angelic sword. But it is a small fear, mitigated by the powerful attraction she feels for him.

"Not entirely. And you do have that mortal commodity called free will—although it's the uncommon mortal that actually exercises it. But you are no common mortal, are you? For that reason, I should like you to accompany me for a time. Would you, fair Braga, spend some of your allotted mortality with me? I can promise great exploits. And perhaps even immortality."

She looks askance down the corridor leading to the Blood Tree— now nothing more than a black silhouette against a faint red glow.

Rahab says, "You needn't be concerned with them. All your worldly allegiances have been negated by my intervention. You are free, Braga of Faery Valley. Free to do as you please."

"Or as *you* please," she demurs. "And if I refuse you?"

"Then you may go back to your mundane schemes and live out your meager days in futility. With no hope of becoming immortal."

"You offer immortality like an apple under a horse's nose. I am no mare."

"No, but you will die and rot in the ground the same as any dumb animal. I offer another way."

"Why? Why me?"

"As I said, we are kin. You are the strong link I need to these mortal worlds. In this physical form, I am attracted to you. I would explore this attraction and experience carnal desire and perhaps achieve that state known as love. I have no such desire for ordinary mortals. They repulse me. You are exceptional, dear Braga."

She looks longingly at the black tree in the strange distance. She tries to weigh the rogue angel's words against everything the monk told her of the coming chaos and advent of evil, but being in the immortal's presence somehow makes this task impossible.

"Here's a tempting apple for you," says Rahab, openly taunting her. "Come with me and we shall take vengeance on those half-human beasts that sacked your village and slaughtered your clan. We won't stop until every last Wulfang is butchered."

"You would make me your whore with bloody vengeance as my payment."

"A whore you could never be. *Consort* comes closer to the truth. Time beckons. What say you?"

"Done," she says. "When the last Wulfang is dead, I will do as you bid."

"Very well. But there is one thing you must do before we set off."

"What one thing?"

Rahab reaches his hand into the white folds of his breast and brings out a handful of glowing smoke. Angelic alchemy forges a great blade out of the smoky heat. It is accomplished in two blinks of the eye, and Rahab holds the sword aloft by its exotically bejeweled haft.

"Take this," he tells her, "and cut down the Blood Tree. Then we shall have your revenge."

Without hesitation, she accepts the radiant sword. It has little weight and she wields it with astounding ease. The sword's dark power courses through the deeper channels of her soul, and she truly believes she is tasting immortality. Glimpses of other worlds and Heavenly dimensions flash before her. A sharp edge of bright awareness prevents her from becoming drunk with the sword's awesome power.

She fixes her eyes on the Blood Tree and all at once she is back on the hazy summit of the Hag, standing before the thick trunk of ancient wood. With a single stroke she fells the tree.

Blood spurts high into the air from the raw stump. The felled tree emits a long piercing scream, and then falls silent.

The monk is aghast. Gragor is mortified by the sight of the terrible blade.

"No!" shouts the monk. "You must not—"

Before she can hear the rest of his words, the angelic sword sweeps her back to Rahab, who takes the sword from her, pulls her to his breast, and spirits her away.

XIII. VENGEANCE

The Wulfang encampment was on high ground overlooking fallow meadows and rocky rills. Some of them danced around a great roaring fire, howling at the moonless sky and shaking their weapons as if taunting distant gods, while others openly fornicated on the campground or gorged on raw meat. Wulfangs too old to fornicate or dance simply watched the revelry with dimming eyes and sneering smiles on their hoary snouts as they recalled bygone nights of their own youthful debaucheries. Fire-shadows danced about the camp like denizens from the Underworld, come to join the revelry.

Belly-down, Rahab and Braga watched from a weedy mound of dank earth.

"There must be more than a hundred of them," she whispered. "Surely some will escape when you attack."

"Stay here and watch," said Rahab. "The next camp will be yours to slay."

Rahab stood to his full height and strode toward the camp. His strides were long and easy, belying the fact that he'd been on earth less than two risings of the sun. Though he wore no clothing, his stippled white skin had the look of finest broadcloth. His long white hair shimmered like glass in the meager light from the Wulfang's bonfire. He held Angel Steel high in his right hand. The blade's glow reminded Braga of the monk's bright cross.

Some of the revelers on the camp's perimeter noticed the striding apparition and howled warnings to the inner camp, their heads thrown back and their haunches low to the ground. Rahab suddenly halted, gripped the sword's haft in both hands and cocked it over his right shoulder. He stood thus for a long moment, as if gauging distances to his many targets. Braga intuited that he was communicating with the sword, commanding the desired degree of power he wanted for his strike. And she knew then that there would be but one strike: one swoop of Angel Steel would fell the entire encampment.

She stood and moved forward for a better view. Her heart thumped hard at her bosom. She tasted vengeance on the night air; it sweetened her breath and set off lustful ripples low in her belly.

As some of the armed Wulfangs charged Rahab, he swung his great sword, its powerful arc describing a thin, curving beam of indigo light. Though the blade made no contact with Wulfang flesh, the arcing beam decanting from the weapon touched them all, sliced through them as if they were made of butter, and cut every one of them into two bloody pieces.

The screams and howls died quickly away, their mournful echoes following to oblivious silence.

"You saw," Rahab said when Braga came to stand at his side.

Unable to speak, she nodded.

"When you are ready to strike, you pour your desire into the weapon and it will do your exact bidding. You see?"

She did.

The next camp was hers.

The Wolf Moon was on the rise, its bright fullness making a stealthy approach all but impossible, but she did not care. She *wanted* these foul descendents of evil shape-shifters to see her coming. She wanted them to see the instrument of their demise in her hand, wanted them to know that Braga of the Heathcoat Clan had come to deal death.

Rahab stood well behind her as she strode into the camp's revelry. She shook her war-braids and unleashed the warbling war cry of her dead clan. In that eerie cry sang the spirits of her mother, her fellow warriors, Tyka and all the rest of her people.

As in the previous camp, the Wulfangs tried to mount a defensive attack. Unfazed by their dangerous proximity, Braga stood with Angel Steel cocked over her shoulder and willed the blade to destroy every half-human creature in the camp.

Then she swung the sword.

The thin bluish shaft of deadly light found every Wulfang in the sprawling encampment and, exactly as she willed it, cut them in two. That she could wield such power was in and of itself astounding, but even more remarkable was that she actually felt the death of each creature the blade's beam touched, felt the terror and the pain and the death of shrunken souls. Dealing wholesale death was dizzying. As Angel Steel reached the end of its arc and every Wulfang lay dead and twitching, Braga counseled herself against becoming drunk with so much power.

She turned back to face Rahab, who held out his hand for the return of his sword. She had no desire to relinquish it. For a dangerous instant, she considered striking the rogue angel with his own harrowing blade. Thomas had said she must steal the sword during the black sun, but she had it now in her hand and had used it to devastating effect through the exertion of her will. Why should she wait to steal it? What would happen if she were to turn it against Rahab now?

"Now you know the true nature of mortality," Rahab said. "And you glimpsed what it means to be immortal, did you not? Wielding an immortal's weapon gives you a taste of godlike power. Do it often enough and you should become immortal yourself. But enough for now. Too much too soon could kill you. Or turn you into a babbling crone."

Reluctantly, she gave up the sword. The instant it left her hand, a great fatigue overcame her and she collapsed in a heap, groaning and gasping for air. When the fatigue left her some time later, she understood how the blade could kill her through injudicious use of it. She needed Rahab to tutor her.

Above all else, she needed to brandish Angel Steel again, and soon.

XIV. PRAYER HOUSE

Mulroy was supposed to be watching his two little sisters while the grownups were in the prayer house for morning worship, but the anthill beneath the bent tree had captured his full notice. A tow-headed boy of ten summers, Mulroy's mind was often off on great imaginary adventures, but this anthill behind the stone prayer house was real, and the army of red ants was his to attack and destroy. With a desultory glance at sisters Hiffa and Heffa, he pulled his makeshift knife from the hemp sash around his waist and attacked the perimeter of the ants' dirt fortress. He'd found the broken bit of blade in a meadow said to be the site of some ancient battle, and fashioned a handle for it by wrapping a tough length of vine around two flat rocks on either side of the blunt end of the steel. Then he sharpened it on a whetstone and knew it was a fine knife. He regretted that he couldn't show off his handiwork for his mum and da, but if they saw it they would take it from him and probably would take turns hiding his rump bloody.

Taking his time, he methodically stabbed the raw earth around the foot of the anthill, each stroke of the blade severing the segmented body of an ant. Now and then he would pause to watch the sundered body of an ant kick its tiny legs in crazy confusion. Mulroy knew he had to be careful in attacking the anthill proper. Hundreds of angry ants would come boiling out of there, ready to counterattack, and if he wasn't vigilant they would swarm up the blade, cover his hand and inflict painful bites. Enough bites from these little bastards and he could die of their poison. And these ants were bigger and more ferocious-looking than any he'd ever seen. It was strange to even find an anthill this time of year. Ants were supposed to be deep underground for their winter sleep, weren't they? And yet this anthill was steaming with mysterious heat. Could these be the Hellfire ants he'd heard about when the elders swapped tall tales around the story-fire? He would have to ask his da about this later.

Thinking a better strategy might be to burn the ants out, Mulroy glanced at his two sisters playing their silly game of hopping stones by the back door of the prayer house. He reckoned he could slip away, run down the trail to his thatched-roof house for his fire-making flint, and then run back here before the girls noticed he'd been gone. They were tattletales and would like nothing better than to see him get a good arse-whipping. With the flints, he could burn kindling on top of the anthill and then watch the fun. He decided it would be worth the risk.

As he stood up to run for home, he saw the white man coming out of the woods on his right. He gaped at the tall figure and decided right away that, no, this wasn't a man at all. This was a giant specter from the Faery realm his mum used to tell him about at bedtime, tales to scare him into the refuge of sleep. He stared at the advancing specter. Mulroy's legs seemed frozen fast to the ground. He wanted to run, to raise the alarm to the adults in the prayer house, but fear held him fast. Though his body was still, his mind was racing, running down possible explanations for why this creature was striding straight for the house of worship.

A tall woman with war braids was standing back at the edge of the woods, hands on her hips and a blank expression on her pretty face. He thought he'd seen her before, but he wasn't sure. The pale creature came on. Now it was holding a sword made of smoke in its upraised right hand, and Mulroy watched in amazement as the smoke solidified and became a glowing blade nearly as long as its bearer was tall.

When the white man was no more than twenty paces away, Mulroy knew at last what he was really seeing: an angel. Like the ones in the picture-prayer books, except that this angel didn't appear to have those great feathery wings. An angel afoot. Bearing a magical sword. Coming straight for him.

A bad angel.

In the picture-prayer-book stories, Angels were either messengers from God or fierce avengers sent to wreak Heavenly havoc upon evildoers. Something—some gruff whispery voice from the lower quarters of his mind—told Mulroy that this wingless angel striding toward him was not here to do the Lord's work. And that trollish voice from below was more often right than not.

When at last he regained control of his legs, Mulroy knew it was too late too run. The bad angel was right on top of him now, holding his sword high in the overcast sky. Mulroy held up his makeshift knife as if it might magically fend off an angel's sword.

And perhaps it did, for the angel did not strike with his sword. Instead, the towering angel reached down a powerful hand and seized Mulroy by the throat and lifted him up so that he was nose-to-nose with the creature, staring into its black eyeballs. Choking and dizzy from lack of breath, Mulroy saw things in those huge black eyes, doorways to terrifying places that couldn't exist in this world—places he hoped he would never have to go.

The angel spoke to him in a deep melodious voice: "I crown you King of the Ants." And then tossed him on top of the anthill. The mound of soft dirt partially collapsed beneath Mulroy's back. Ants swarmed over him, hundreds of tiny mandibles attacking his flesh, inflicting fiercely stinging bites and making him scream, but as soon as he opened his mouth the ants swarmed into it and started biting his tongue, the sides of his mouth, the back of his throat. His scream became a dry gurgling whimper. He knew he had to get up and run or else die from the poison, but he couldn't move. The bad angel had done something to him to freeze him in place as still as a toppled stone statue. His head was angled to one side so that he could glimpse through the segmented bodies swarming over his eyes the fate of his small sisters. He saw what the angel did to them, but his pain prevented the sight from taking hold in his mind; it was a small and rare blessing that he didn't go to his death with any real understanding of the terror his siblings must've felt just before the angel skewered them both on the end of his shining sword and held them up, limp and bloodied, as if showing them to God.

Shock soon made Mulroy oblivious to his body's agony. He saw but didn't really *see* the angel swing his sword and slice off the top of the stone prayer house and flip it into the air with the ease of a man flipping the lid off an earthen jar. He heard but didn't really *hear* the panicked screams of the grownups inside the building. With the disorienting detachment known only to the dying, Mulroy saw the bad angel jam the six-foot-tall iron cross from the prayer-house into the nether regions of the prayer master and then pound the other end of the cross into the ground to make a blasphemous display of the holy man's grisly impalement.

Mulroy's vision quickly dimmed as the ants ate away the filmy surface of his eyes, but by that time his mind had already preceded his body into the realm of the dead.

XV. OVERTURES TO LORD LUCIFER

"Are your delicate sensibilities offended?" asked Rahab. This time he'd used Angel Steel as a more or less ordinary sword, slashing torsos and hacking off limbs of the Christ Cult worshippers until every one of them was mercilessly slaughtered. He'd chivvied them out of the prayer house, lined them up in the churchyard and done for them one by one. As before, Braga had watched passively, seemingly as a disinterested spectator. And now that it was over, Rahab was piling the dismembered remains in the center of the graveyard, arranging them in mysterious symmetry beyond Braga's understanding.

"My sensibilities are not so delicate," she finally answered, "but I fail to see what this butchery accomplishes. Senseless slaughter is all I see. You've sacked six of these prayer houses, but to what end? To offend your God with your childish temper tantrums?"

"Ah. But there is much you cannot see. Giving offense to the Father is not my main concern, though I admit I do rather enjoy that aspect of it." Rahab tore the head of a young woman with straw-colored hair from her bloodied shoulders and placed it atop the head of a stone angel in the center of the cemetery. "This butchery I do to honor Lord Lucifer. If I am to be admitted to his realm, I must make the appropriate overtures and ritualistic offerings."

"So your aim is to visit him in Hell." Braga recalled the monk's prediction that Rahab would enlist the denizens of Hell in his war against God's Heavenly fortress. She remembered as well his charging her with the task of stealing Angel Steel during the black sun and striking Rahab a crippling blow with it, to forestall an apocalyptic conflict. She said, "To get his permission to join forces with the other fallen angels and rally them to wage your mad war."

"Perhaps you see more than I thought. Yes. You had the ever so *wise* counsel of the sorcerer monk. And you did drink of the Blood Tree." Rahab fixed his black eyes upon her. She felt a chill to her bones. Rahab continued: "My kind are sometimes called 'the many-eyed ones' because we are capable of seeing so much of Creation. You think I do not see through your plan to steal my sword and strike me a devastating blow? The sorcerer's plan is not entirely faulty, but it has one major flaw. That flaw being that you are going to accompany me to Hell to meet the Dark Lord Lucifer. I assure you that such a meeting will dash all hope of subverting my will or his. If he allows you to leave, you will do so as Lucifer's loyal servant. There is no other way."

"Suppose I refuse to go with you?" Her fearful heart raced as she suggested such open defiance.

Rahab laughed, dislodging a shower of leaves from the tall trees at the back edge of the churchyard. "I will not force you to do anything. I will not have to. Do you not see? Angel Steel has its claim on you. You have wielded my bewitching blade, and now it owns you. You would follow it even to Hell."

Rahab offered her the sword's haft. "Try with all your will not to take it," he challenged.

Even as her right hand went toward the sword, Braga tried to call it back, to resist accepting the weapon. Her long fingers stopped just short of touching the thick pommel. Her hand trembled. She stared at the softly glowing blade and at the remaining drops of blood that the otherworldly alloy hadn't yet absorbed, hating its hold on her and at the same time yearning to take it in hand and feel its sublime power coursing through her body and soul. Cursing softly, she closed her hand around its hilt and took Angel Steel into her temporal possession.

Rahab was right. She would follow him and his bewitching blade anywhere, even into the innards of Hell. And beyond.

XVI. ENTERING HELL

"Hell has many doorways," Rahab said, standing upon low, rocky ground. "I favor this one because it is the place where the so-called Messiah was put to death."

They were outside the city walls of an ancient place called Jerusalem. Only moments ago, Rahab had enfolded Braga in his arms, held her tightly to his breast and instantaneously transported her to one of those other worlds the monk had spoken of, a world she'd never before entered.

"Some call this the Place of Skulls, or Golgotha," he explained. "It was little more than a cesspool, a foul sump where bodies were dumped and where death reined with a bony fist. Now, of course, the place is revered by the faithful followers of Christ. What do you suppose they would think if they knew an entrance to Hell hides here?"

She shook her head. She hugged Angel Steel to her bosom as if cradling a beloved child in her arms. She only half-heard Rahab's words. In ringing whispers the sword spoke to her in a language foreign to her ears, but it nevertheless soothed her troubled soul. At some deep level of understanding, her soul communed with the sword and intuited its esoteric message.

"Now give me the sword and I shall open the way," he told her.

She reluctantly relinquished the weapon and immediately felt within her chest an aching absence that became wrenching despair. She whimpered.

Rahab held the blade high as if pointing a bright, accusing finger at the Heavens. He said words in the same language the sword had whispered and then suddenly plunged the blade into the ground. A wide radius of ground around the embedded blade began to quake. Then it began to smoke and glow red with heat. Rahab pulled the blade from the disturbed earth and stepped back.

The radius roiled as it became molten sludge with a steamy

reddish-black blush. Braga recoiled from the heat, but Rahab seemed unaffected by it. He turned, held out his arm to her, and she went to him, desperate to be closer to Angel Steel—and perhaps to him as well. For the moment, she couldn't distinguish between the lure of the blade and the power Rahab seemed to exert over her.

Huddled against him under his powerful arm, she was somehow protected from the scorching heat. She watched in rapt wonder as a single bubble slowly rose from the pool of heaving lava and expanded to the size of the mouth of a large cave. She saw her reflection in the bubble's pinkish surface, momentarily taken aback by her dwarfish size in relation to the angel—and by the look of raw hunger on her haggard face. *Gods, what am I becoming?* she wondered.

The bubble continued to swell, its membranous skin quivering spasmodically. She feared it might pop and blister her with fiery dew.

"The way is opened," said Rahab. "Stay close to me."

And he suddenly strode forward, whisking her along, and the bubble-like membrane moved with them into a suspended antechamber of red Hell. Inside the bubble the air was surprisingly chilled.

The protective bubble sank, taking them into the lava pool and then descended deeper into darkness. Moments later, it emerged from the darkness and drifted lazily through smoky air above a strange red landscape.

Seen through the concave inner surface of the pink sphere, Lucifer's demesne was a phantasmagorical scene from some tortured soul's nightmare. Braga could not have dreamed up anything so ominously disturbing as what she saw below. Everywhere she looked she saw raw, red earth, veined with black runnels that might've been conveying demonic ichor to the dark lords of Hell. Steam rose from jagged fissures in the rocky ground. A malevolent haze hung over everything. There was no sky; instead, there was a great overarching dome of reddish-orange rock. The bubble drifted above the eerily menacing landscape and finally touched down before a footbridge made of human skulls. The cobbled heads of bone formed an arched walkway over a moat of flowing lava. A tall, thin figure robed in scarlet stood in the middle of the footbridge.

The bubble silently burst and left Braga and Rahab standing upon the hot ground before the entrance to the bridge of skulls. Now she could see more clearly. She saw that the figure on the bridge wasn't wearing a scarlet robe at all; rather, the figure was made of undulating fire—fire in the shape of a man.

In a voice as dry as scorching desert winds, the fire-man spoke: *"Hell from beneath is moved for thee to meet thee at thy coming; it stirreth up the dead for thee, even all the chief ones of the earth; it hath raised up from their thrones all the kings of the nations. All they shall speak, and say unto thee, Art thou also become as weak as we? Art thou become like unto us?"*

"Quote not the words of that addled-brain prophet Isaiah to me," Rahab said in a booming voice. "Stand aside and let us pass. I am Rahab the Wrathful, self-exiled from Heaven. Stand aside or know my wrath!"

The man made of oily flames laughed an oily laugh, then turned, bent over and farted. Belching fire shot forth from his hindquarters to lick the air in front of Braga's face. The stench of charred bowels nearly sickened her.

"Pass then," the fire-man intoned officiously as he stood erect once more. "Cross over into my Lord's kingdom and see how far your wrath will take you, rebellious Rahab."

Without hesitation, Rahab and Braga stepped onto the footbridge of skulls spanning the molten moat and entered Hell.

XVII. THE BOY

As they stepped off the skulls and onto raw ground, Braga saw what appeared to be a garden of mossy stones set in a depression of ocher earth. Upon closer examination, she realized that the moss was hair and the rounded stones were human heads. Hundreds of them. The owners of those heads were buried up to their necks in black sludge, their jaws unhinged so that the liquid filth flowed into their mouths and down their throats, keeping them all in a perpetual state of choking and gagging on the foul sludge. A gargling hum arose from the tortured heads, creating a discordant harmony.

"Who are they?" she asked.

"Hell's choir," said Rahab. "Lord Lucifer has quite the sense of humor, does he not? He mocks the Father at every opportunity."

"I'm not laughing." The stench of the black sludge made her gag. "Let's get away from the poor sods. Which way do we go?"

"We go across them."

"Across…those?"

"Yes. Use them as steppingstones. It's the only way."

"You've been here before?"

"No. But I recognize patterns, signs and portents, and I know this way leads to the one we seek. I sense his presence and know we are close."

"So it takes a fallen angel to find a fallen angel," she posited. Before their descent into Hell, Rahab had told her of Lucifer's banishment from Heaven and of the fallen angels that followed the resentful exile.

"I did not *fall.* I chose to leave. I was not driven out. I flew from that wretched place."

Braga was no longer listening to Rahab. She was looking at a small boy sitting atop a mound of red, porous dirt in front of an outcropping of orange rock. She recognized him as the boy Rahab had thrown onto the anthill—the boy who had died of countless ant bites. The last time she'd seen him, his face was so swollen and envenomed that it didn't look at all human. Now, however, his face looked as it had before the angry ants attacked it. Death had been kind to him.

Then she suddenly understood. "You sent him here," she said. "That boy."

"Yes. We come bearing a gift, a relatively untainted soul for Lord Lucifer."

They trod upon the disharmonious heads, stepping from one to another until they were across the stinking swamp of black sewage. By the time they stepped onto the ground on the other side, the gargling choir's volume had increased tenfold, seemingly amplified by their passage over them.

The boy stood up to greet them with an intensely unhappy coun-tenance. He'd obviously been crying, but now he appeared on the verge of an emotional explosion.

"What's your name, boy?" asked Braga.

"Why did you make me come here?" the boy ejaculated, waving his arms.

"Never mind that," she said. "Your name?"

He looked at the ground and muttered, "Mulroy." He looked accusingly at Rahab. "You fed me to the ants."

"Yes, I did. And I sent you on ahead of us, to prepare the way."

"I don't like it here," Mulroy muttered. Then he raised his voice: "I wanna go home."

"You won't be here long," Rahab assured the boy. "I promise."

"Where's me sisters? Me mum and da?"

Braga knelt in front of him and placed a hand on his shoulder. "They're in a better place."

"I wanna go there. Can't I go where they are?"

"We'll see," she said, looking askance at Rahab.

"Come along, lad," Rahab said. "We're going to meet someone very important. You should be honored."

"Who?" Mulroy asked with a hopeful expression.

"The high king of this low place," answered the angel. "Lucifer."

"The Devil?!" The boy stiffened.

"So some call him. He is like me, but more powerful. You needn't fear him."

Braga held her silence. She thought it was Rahab the boy should fear, but there was no point in telling him that, not now. She took the boy's hand and together they fell in behind Rahab, who was already moving along a narrow footpath of shiny black granite snaking upward beside a rivulet of steaming lava and into rocky red foothills.

"It is beautiful here, is it not?" said Rahab. "The surface of your planet was much like this four billion of your years ago. Raging fires, vast rivers of molten rock and beautiful billows of steam. I should've kept it just that way, had I been the Father, but of course He had other plans. He had to make the planet habitable for your kind."

"You don't care much for us mortals," she said, pulling the boy along to keep him up with her long strides.

"Care? It is not my nature to care. I am intrigued by mortals' souls, though. You inhabit your physical bodies and live your short lives upon the earth, but you seem unaware that your souls connect you to infinite realms of spirit. Those that do sense the presence of their souls think the soul is within the body, but the soul is most certainly without—which is why it goes on without the body, when the carcass is rotting in the ground. How can a thinking species be so ignorant, so blind to truth? How can you neglect to use those big brains in your skulls? Most of you waste the gift you've been given. Human life is not so different from the lives of those ants this boy amused himself with. You have much in common with the ants. You scurry after the same things. You concern yourselves mainly with food, shelter, sensory gratification, procreation. And like the ants, you make war with dedicated ferocity. War is what man does best. I *do* admire that. But you mortals could be so much more. If you let your spirit lead you, you could rise up from the muck, from your human anthills, perhaps to find your place in the higher realms. But most of you have no inkling those realms even exist."

"So you do care," she said. "Care enough to judge us and condemn our ignorant ways."

Rahab laughed. "No, woman, I don't condemn. I am merely making observations. I should leave the condemnation to Lord Lucifer and the Father Most High."

Braga said, "But you condemned this boy to death, and now you intend to sacrifice his mortal soul to gain the favor of Lucifer."

Mulroy tightened his grip on her hand, as if to admonish her for mentioning his name to the ruthless angel.

"The boy's soul is a gift, nothing more. One does not approach the Lord of the underworld empty-handed. It is simply not done. Little Mulroy should be honored to have his pitiful soul accepted by Lord Lucifer."

"Destroyed. His soul will be destroyed, won't it?"

"Of course. But to good purpose. If all goes well, Lucifer will devour the boy's soul. Perhaps a small portion of it will live on in Lucifer. Of that I am not certain. But I know this: If Lucifer refuses our gift, then he may destroy us all."

Panicked by what he'd just heard, Mulroy yanked his hand from

Braga's grasp, turned and started running back the way they'd come.

Mulroy ran for his soul's life. He hadn't been sure he had one until he absorbed enough of the killer angel's words to become convinced that he must have a soul—one Lucifer would relish as a delicacy the way Mulroy's da used to relish the roasted balls of slaughtered lambs. Was this body that was now carrying him over the red ground his soul? He knew his other body had died on the anthill, and that a hungry darkness had swallowed him up and shat him out in Hell, so how could it be that he now had a new body? Mayhap this was his Hell-body—but nobody had ever told him of such. It was more than his juvenile mind could grasp. But the main thing now was to stay out of the grasp of the murdering angel who would give him over to the Devil.

So he ran and ran.

Into the hands of the Devil.

Mulroy tried to scream but no sound came out of the O of his mouth. The Devil lifted him up the way a father will sometimes hold an infant high overhead as if offering it to the sky or to the gods beyond.

"WHAT A FINE SWEET SOUL," the Devil said in a booming voice that hurt Mulroy's ears.

"Please," he said, finding his voice in desperation, "don't eat me, Good Lord."

Lucifer smiled. He set the boy back on his feet and gazed down at him with huge black eyes.

Mulroy took in the awesome aspect of the Lord of Hell. Lucifer's smooth skin—if skin it was—was the whitest white Mulroy had ever seen, but in places it reflected the reddish-orange light of the sur-rounding Hellscape so that parts of him appeared red. Lucifer was at least three heads taller than the killer angel, and handsomer as well. Mulroy had never before seen such a handsome creature. His shoulders were broad and powerful, his abdomen thickly ribbed with muscle, and muscular legs depended from narrow hips. Between those brawny legs his cock hung well below his knees, reminding Mulroy of the ground-dragging cocks he'd seen on shaggy ponies in rutting season. Though he didn't understand why, he was suddenly terrified of that dangling cock and of what it might do to him if the Devil took such a dirty notion.

"Greetings, Lord Lucifer," said the killer angel as he came up behind Mulroy. "I am Rahab, late of the hierarchical choir and the harmonious wheel. I cast myself out of the crystal empire and am come before you now with this mortal offering."

"RAHAB, WELCOME TO MY HUMBLE DEMENSE. I ACCEPT YOUR FINE OFFERING AND THANK YOU FOR THE COURTESY."

Mulroy could not take his eyes from the Devil's cock. Was it getting bigger? Sweet Jesu, it was!

Rahab came forward to stand beside Mulroy. He bowed his head to the Devil.

"BUT WHO IS THIS FAIR LADY IN YOUR WAKE?" Lucifer's dark eyes seemed to pierce the tall woman called Braga.

Mulroy wanted to clasp his hands over his ears because Lucifer booming voice was so painful to hear, but he didn't do it for fear of giving offense.

"She is Braga of the slaughtered clan of Heathcoat," Rahab said with a flourish of slender hands. "My consort in the realm of men."

"YOU HAVE NOT YET STOLEN HER FLOWER."

"I am saving her for the right moment." Rahab lowered his chin in deference. "But she is yours, Lord, should you desire."

Lucifer folded his massive arms across his chest. "THANK YOU, NO. I THINK SHE IS DESTINED FOR A HIGHER PURPOSE. BUT YOU WANT SOMETHING OF ME, COUSIN. I KNOW YOU DIDN'T COME HERE TO JOIN MY NOBLE LEGIONS."

"Heaven is ripe for the picking. I have come to tell you how you can shake the Father's tree."

Lucifer's sudden outburst of booming laughter sent Mulroy to his knees in agony. He feared his skull would crack open like a hen's egg and his brains would leak out like runny yolk.

"I speak true," Rahab said with anger rising in his voice. "Before I left, I sowed much dissention in the choirs. They are vulnerable as they have never been before."

Lucifer's laughter broke off, much to Mulroy's relief. "I HAVE WARRED AGAINST HEAVEN AND SUFFERED HUMILIATING DEFEAT. I WILL NOT DO SO AGAIN."

"But this time you could win. You could steal a great victory and adorn yourself in eternal glory."

"YOU PRESUME MUCH, RAHAB, BOTH OF ME AND HIS HOLY HIGHNESS."

"Forgive me, Lord. I only—"

"ENOUGH OF THIS TALK OF WAR. PERHAPS WE WILL RETURN TO IT LATER. NOW I SHALL HAVE THIS FINE OFFERING YOU HAVE BROUGHT ME."

Lucifer turned his dark gaze upon Mulroy. The Devil's face glowed red with Hell-light. His horse-sized cock began to redden and rise. The boy blanched and trembled violently at the approach of his eternal doom.

XVII. THE BLACK SUN

Braga's mind raced to find some course of action that might save the boy's soul, but her desperate thoughts succeeded only in running futile circles within her skull that made her dizzy.

Damn that mist-walking monk! His mad plan was a shambles now. How could she steal Angel Steel during the black of the sun when she was in an infernal place where there *was* no sun? *I curse you, Mist Walker. I curse you and your impotent Cross Cult god.*

Then she looked into Lucifer's face and shuddered, awed by his splendor, but she felt something more—a deep-down suspicion that she was looking into a false-face. She could almost see the thing lurking beneath the handsome countenance but its true aspect would not resolve itself clearly enough to be seen. She thought the sap of the Blood Tree must have given her the ability to see that there was something—something incredibly hideous—hiding behind the smooth fleshy mask of perfect beauty. She looked away, suddenly afraid that if she saw Lucifer's true face, she would turn to stone or ash.

Lucifer's gigantic prick was standing straight out from his loins now, jutting at the boy like a deadly lance. The boy was fear-frozen, as if spellbound by the grotesque erection aiming its single slit of an eye at his small round face.

Gods, if I had the angel's sword I would lop off that throbbing beast.

"And die for your troubles," a voice whispered in her right ear.

Braga turned right, but there was no sign of the whisperer. She thought for a moment that she must have been losing her mind to this stifling landscape of Hell.

"No," said the disembodied voice, "you are not losing your mind. I am with you."

She whispered, "Mist Walker?"

"Yes. The eclipse is beginning. The black sun. You must reach into the angel's chest and seize the sword. Count to one hundred, then do it."

When she responded neither with her lips nor her thoughts, Thomas said, "You do know how to count, don't you?"

Yes, you bloody fool, I can count.

"Good. Start now."

She began counting in her head. She moved closer to Rahab—close enough to reach into his chest and steal the smoking light that would become Angel Steel. If Thomas was wrong and it didn't play out the way he'd said it would, she would likely end up dead—or worse. Much worse.

Rahab's attention was fixed on the boy. He seemed to be enjoying Mulroy's terror, feeding off it like a starving vagabond at a banquet table. Lucifer moved closer to the boy, no doubt savoring the young soul he was about to devour. His monstrous prick had turned an unpleasant purple, shot through with splotches of black and resembling the infected flesh around a canker, ripe and ready to explode and spew bloody pus.

Geysers of fire erupted from swollen craters that rose like fleshy bumps from the landscape behind Lucifer.

Twenty-six...twenty-seven...Are you sure this will work, Mist Walker?

Thomas did not answer. Braga counted faster.

The Hellscape grew eyes. Countless faces appeared in the red rock. Red-tinted steam filled the air. All eyes were on the boy, the sacrifice. Lucifer's domain was rife with unsavory expectancy.

Lucifer's hideous organ began to stretch and then twined like a giant snake about Mulroy's torso, pinning his arms to his sides.

Fifty-one....fifty-two...

Rahab began to laugh at the unseemly spectacle of the Devil's prick encircling the boy and snaking around his little neck; but his laughter sounded hollow. Braga thought he was slyly mocking the Ruler of Hell—a dangerous and foolish thing to do, because Lucifer was surely slyer than Rahab. It occurred to her then that the rogue angel was truly mad, drunk on his own wrathful rebellion and swollen ambitions. No matter. She would soon bring an end to his rebellion by striking him a crippling blow with his own sword. She steeled herself for the task, knowing she had little to lose now that she was trapped in the underworld. She did not allow herself to think about how Lord Lucifer might react to her smiting Rahab. Not that she could do anything about it.

Seventy-eight...seventy-nine...

Now the head of Lucifer's prick hung over Mulroy's head like a serpent poised to strike its prey, undulating to the subtle beat of hellish heartlessness. The slit in its tip stretched open like a large mouth and revealed a whitish lining slick with dripping mucus. The boy's eyes widened with new terror as he looked up at the serpent-prick's widening maw. Lucifer held his massive arms straight out to either side, as if he were crucified. Mocking the Cross Cult's storied hero.

Braga glanced at Rahab and saw a white radiance within his chest. Angel Steel. Was the black sun somehow making it glow?

The serpent-prick's mouth engulfed Mulroy's head and slid down toward his shoulders with a sickening slippery-slick sound.

Ninety-two...ninety-three...Bugger this!

Braga hooked her right hand, swung around and plunged it into Rahab's glowing chest, hitting the exact spot he'd always reached into to bring out his terrible weapon. Her rigid fingers broke through a thin, brittle surface and sank into dry flesh soft as duck's down.

Rahab's face registered angelic surprise—which is to say, he looked a lot like a man Braga had once decapitated in battle, his face forming a disbelieving expression when his head rolled to a halt on the ground and beheld its headless body spouting blood from the stump of the neck. But Rahab's surprise quickly became bellowing rage.

Braga withdrew her hand and held high the glowing ball of smoke. It was neither hot nor cool. It was weightless, yet surprisingly solid. A tingling current ran up her arm. A wave of raw lust wracked her body. The smoke began to curl, swirl, twine, lengthen…seductively slither…

Rahab's shoulders curved inward, spooning his chest. His long hands came up to clutch at his breast. Even as he cringed in unmistakable pain, his black eyes fixed murderously on the woman who'd stolen his magnificent sword.

"Give me that!" Rahab bellowed. He dropped to one knee, clutching his chest with one hand and reaching out for the weapon with the other.

The glowing smoke in Braga's hand finally took the shape of the great sword and began to solidify. It took on such weight that she feared it was becoming too heavy for her arm to support it, but then she felt a surge of strength-giving energy flowing into her, and the weapon became an extension of her body, melded with her flesh through its own alchemical magic. Her female parts suddenly ached with lust and went wet and slippery with uncanny wanting.

"Now," Mist Walker's disembodied voice whispered with desperate urgency.

Braga held the haft of the sword with both her hands, cocked it over her shoulder and swung it with all her strength. The blade struck Rahab's left shoulder and sliced diagonally through his torso, coming out just above his right hip. There was a blinding flash of light and a deafening clap of thunder. Braga's whole body vibrated, thrumming in tune with the blade. An orgasmic wave broke deliciously within her tingling loins and she was panting like a hot puppy.

The blow would've cut a mortal in half, but Rahab's physical form remained intact. There was no blood, no sign of wounded flesh. But then the path the blade had taken through his body began to leak silver light, and Braga knew he *was* bleeding.

Rahab began to shrink, to shrivel. Before her eyes he dwindled until he became a dwarfish little troll with a repulsive face and arms too long for his stumpy body. His knuckles dragged the ground as he rambled about in confused circles. He gibbered like the mummer's flea-bitten monkey Braga had seen once in Ox Ford.

Braga turned toward Lucifer and cocked the sword over her shoulder again. "Release the boy," she said. "Let him go or I'll slice off your ugly snake."

"Braga, no!" Mist Walker's voice was a faraway echo.

Then Lucifer showed her his true face.

XVIII. THE DARK BOND

In his face Braga saw all the things mortals abhor. The pale under-bellies of crawling things that feed on decaying flesh. The spilled innards of proud warriors dying on the battlefield. The disfiguring torment of a mother who's lost her child to disease or to stupidity. The harsh disinterest of the storm that destroys a village. The hate and fear of one race for another. The seething selfishness that hides in the heart's secret chambers. The lust in a lecher's eyes as he gazes upon innocent young children. The unspoken belief that all gods are brutal predators.

All these things and more she saw in the unmasked face before her. And the worst of it was that Lucifer never shed his outward beauty. The evil showed through the pleasing contours of his beatific countenance. Only his eyes changed: They became the dead eyes of a vulture feeding on carrion and human debris.

Lucifer's shape-shifting prick disgorged Mulroy's shoulders and head, and then uncoiled and retracted into the high arch of his groin until it was only a reddish knob with a small glittering eye. The slimed boy fell to the ground, eyes rolling up in his skull.

"YOU MUST GIVE ME SOMETHING IN RETURN FOR SPARING THIS BOY'S SOUL."

Still poised to strike with the stolen blade, Braga said, "I'll give you a taste of this Heavenly blade, you stinking Devil!"

"YOU THINK I FEAR THAT LITTLE SWORD? YOU GREATLY AMUSE ME, WOMAN. BUT I DO ADMIRE YOUR FOOLISH COURAGE. I THINK YOU WILL SERVE ME VERY WELL."

"Serve you? I will never serve the likes of you."

Rahab the troll began to flog his own stumpy prick, gibbering louder and running in new aimless circles.

"THE CHOICE IS YOURS, BRAGA OF THE HEATHCOAT CLAN, LATE OF FAERY VALLEY. WILL YOU RETURN TO THE WORLD OF MEN AS MY INSTRUMENT, OR WILL YOU REMAIN HERE AS SISTER TO MY LITTLE TROLL RAHAB, YOURSELF AN UGLY LITTLE TROLL?"

Faint but clear in her right ear, the voice of Mist Walker: "You should not have challenged him. Now he will hold you in his dark bond forever."

Ignoring the sorcerer's words, she said, "Come then, you evil prick. Come against my sword if you dare!" She knew she was risking everything with her brazen behavior, but Angel Steel had infused her with a warrior's deadly assurance—and with unquenched bloodlust. The battle fury was upon her as never before.

"SO BE IT. YOU ARE DRUNK WITH UNACCUSTOMED POWER AND MUST SEE FOR YOURSELF THAT THIS PUNY BLADE DOES NOT MAKE YOU INVINCIBLE. STRIKE ME, BITCH! STRIKE ME AND BE DAMNED!"

She struck without hesitation and with all her might. Angel Steel sang as it sliced through Lucifer's abdomen from hip to hip.

To no effect.

She'd just as well have been slicing air for all the good it did.

Undaunted and fiercely determined, she struck again, this time driving the blade into his ridged belly. Again the blade met no resistance, had no effect.

"Damn you!" she said through clenched teeth.

"I WAS DAMNED AEONS AGO," Lucifer said, almost singing the words. "BUT I THANK YOU FOR THE SENTIMENT. NOW DO YOU SEE YOU CANNOT WOUND ME? THIS PHYSICAL FORM IS BUT A SUIT OF CLOTHING. MY TRUE ESSENCE IS

ELSEWHERE AND NOWHERE. STRIKE ALL YOU WISH. I AM IMPERVIOUS TO YOUR FOOLHARDY ASSAULT."

Braga struck once more, thinking—hoping—that the third strike would have some numerical magic behind it because 3 had been considered an auspicious number by her people.

But it did not. The blade sang harmlessly through Lucifer's massive thigh.

"ENOUGH OF THIS FOLLY. NOW YOU MUST CHOOSE. WILL YOU SERVE ME TO SPARE THE BOY AND YOURSELF? IF YOU SAY YES, YOU WILL HAVE COMPLETE AUTONOMY IN THE WORLD OF MEN. YOU WILL BE MY SECRET EMISSARY."

Resigned to the fact that she could not make this Devil bleed, Braga let the sword hang limply to the ground. "I don't understand. What are you telling me?"

"I WILL SEND YOU INTO THE MORTAL WORLD WITH YOUR STOLEN BLADE, YOUR BOY AND YOUR FREEDOM. WHAT YOU DO THERE WILL BE OF YOUR OWN CHOOSING. I WILL BE WATCHING YOUR…PROGRESS. YOU SEE, BRAGA, FOR ALL YOUR STERLING INTENTIONS, YOU WILL PLAY HAVOC UPON THE WORLD. YOU WITH YOUR BLADE WILL BE MY GLORIOUS LITTLE SONG SUNG IN SIZZLING BLOOD. PUT SIMPLY, YOU WILL BE MY LITTLE TOY. OR YOU CAN RE-FUSE MY OFFER AND REMAIN HERE AS MY LITTLE TROLL. AND I WILL DEVOUR THE BOY'S SWEET SOUL."

"So I have no choice. I see your game." She pointed the blade it him. "You twist words and their meanings to suit your evil purpose. But I will prove you wrong. I will use this sword to vanquish your earthly minions. I WILL NOT BE YOUR PLAYTHING!"

"AH, THAT'S THE SPIRIT. I KNEW YOU WOULD NOT DIS-APPOINT ME." Lucifer came closer to her. He reached down and seized one of her war-braids. "TO SEAL OUR BOND WE WILL EXCHANGE GIFTS. I TAKE THIS BRAID OF YOUR LOVELY HAIR…"

He sliced off the braid with a long fingernail.

"…AND GIVE YOU THIS." Lucifer made a shrill whistling sound with his sensuous lips, and a firebird flew out of the nearest crater of fire. It circled overhead until its flames died out, and then it swooped down to land on Lucifer's broad shoulder and cast a sinister gaze upon Braga.

It was the biggest raven she had ever seen, but even more striking than its size was its color. "A white raven," she said with wonder. The *whitest* white she'd ever seen. It was even whiter than Rahab's flesh had been before she turned him into a reddish troll, and whiter than Lucifer's false form. It had bright pink eyes that seemed to glow with furious intelligence. She withered under its piercing gaze. Angel Steel slipped from her grip and clattered on the hard ground.

"KRAKE WILL BE MY EYES IN THE WORLD. EVEN WHEN YOU DO NOT SEE HIM, HE AND I WILL SEE YOU. NOTHING YOU DO WILL ESCAPE KRAKE'S NOTICE. YOU CANNOT KILL HIM, SO DON'T WASTE TIME TRYING."

"Bugger you and your albino raven," Braga said through her fatigue.

"KRAKE WILL BE A WINGED REMINDER OF YOUR BOND TO ME. YOUR CURSES ROLL OFF HIS FEATHERED BREAST LIKE RAIN, SO SAVE YOUR LABORED BREATH."

She turned her back on Lucifer and went to the boy. She knelt beside him and lightly slapped his cheeks until he rose up, groggy but revived.

"Whu—" Mulroy's question faltered. He looked up at the white raven perched on Lucifer's shoulder. The boy's eyes grew wide. He stood and picked up a piece of red quartz and pegged it at the bird. The stone struck the raven's breast and bounced off. The raven flew straight down at Mulroy and the boy fell on his rear with a yelp of surprise. The bird landed on Mulroy's chest and scolded the boy with shrill squawks. "He'll peck out me eyes!"

Krake ripped a strip of flesh from Mulroy's cheek, leaving a bloodless gash. Then the raven cawed three times and took to the sulfurous air.

"KRAKE HAS A TASTE FOR DEAD FLESH," Lucifer warned the boy. "BUT UNLESS YOU ANTAGONIZE HIM FURTHER, HE'LL LEAVE YOU BE."

Braga picked up Angel Steel and felt an immediate surge of

renewing energy from it. "So I'm to return to the world with your annoying raven and a dead boy. And so burdened, I am to amuse you with my ventures. So be it. But mark me well, Devil. I wager I'll have a few surprises for you."

"I HAVE NO DOUBT," said Lucifer.

Then he laughed boisterously, and Hell quaked.

XIX. ANGEL STEEL

Thomas sits atop Hag Mountain, glumly waiting for Braga to reappear. His prescience informed him that this is the place she will reenter the world, but when he tries to divine what manner of woman she will return as, he draws a blank.

He fears she may come back as something utterly demonic, something so hammered and warped on the forge of Hell as to be scarcely recognizable as human.

She should not have challenged Lucifer, he laments. *I should've warned her sooner than I did. Whatever evil he's done to her, it rests squarely on my head and heavy on my heart. If she slays me with Angel Steel, it will be my just reward.*

He sits cross-legged before the charred stump of the Blood Tree. The stump gives off a red glow, illuminating the thick mist. The air is charged with expectancy, as if anticipating the coming of something momentous. Surely something diabolical. Thomas shudders within his cloak. He pulls the cowl over his head. He waits. And waits.

Out of the timeless mists she comes striding on strong legs, the dead boy in tow. A huge white raven glides down out of nowhere and lights on the charred stump. The raven caws three times and fixes its cold pink eyes hungrily upon Thomas.

"Mist Walker," Braga says with a solemn nod. Angel Steel is sheathed on her back, its haft jutting up behind her left shoulder.

Relieved that her appearance hasn't changed, except that her hair is now as white as his and one of her war braids is missing, Thomas returns her nod. "Have you come to kill me?"

"Why should I kill you?" she asks with a hint of amusement.

Thomas shrugs. "For meddling in angelic affairs. For using you as my foil against the powers of darkness. I don't imagine Lucifer appreciated my sticking my nose in."

"I don't believe Lord Lucifer was interested in you or in making war on Heaven. He seemed happy to have Rahab as his new monkey-demon. And even happier to have me as *his* foil."

"So you *have* come to do Lucifer's work." Thomas regarded the white raven. "And this unnatural bird is his spy?"

"Lucifer sees with Krake's eyes. But I do as I please. I am my own agent. The buggering Devil thinks I'm his plaything. I intend to prove otherwise, now that Angel Steel is mine."

"And the boy?" Thomas nods at the living dead boy who is standing demurely in Braga's shadow.

"It seems I'm to be saddled with him and forced to endure his stench as a reminder that I am mortal. It was the only way I could save the boy's soul from destruction."

"So now his walking corpse and pitiful soul belong to you."

"So it seems."

Thomas stands. "I see," he says. "You are gaming Lucifer. You are his game-piece but you make your own moves."

"Well put, Mist Walker." She smiles. "And you are going to help me play the game."

"How so?" He pushes back his cowl and his white hair falls free about his shoulders.

"You're the sorcerer," she says with a half-smile. "You tell me."

Braga, Thomas and the dead boy walked out of the mist and into a strange landscape crisscrossed by hard roads painted with yellow streaks and curved arrows. They moved cautiously through angular canyons formed by massive glass-and-steel towers reaching high into the starless night sky. Unnatural lights glowed everywhere. Shiny horseless carriages ran smoothly over the maze of roads, each one emitting odd whirring sounds and odder odors that reminded Braga of the fire-pits of Hell.

"What *is* this place, Mist Walker?" she asked as she placed a hand on his shoulder. "Have you spirited us back to Hell?"

He was perplexed. "I don't know. This is not the place we should've come to. This is…" His voice trailed off when two men in bizarre garb appeared on the stone walkway ahead. "This is all wrong. The Hag must've misplaced us. I think we've traveled to a…different time."

"We can do that?"

"So it would seem."

Mulroy gawked at strangely dressed women frozen behind great sheets of brightly-lit glass. "We better get outta here," he said, "or we could end up like them poor ladies."

The two men on the blocky walkway were coming closer, and now they noticed the three intruders. The stouter one said something that sounded like, "I didn't know it was hallowing."

The other man laughed, but his laughter quickly ended when he caught wind of Mulroy's dead flesh. "Good God," he said, "don't you people ever bathe?"

"The homeless have costume parties?" asked the stout one, chuckling.

The two men scurried across the street to get away from them, dodging the humming carriages. Some of the carriages honked like sick geese.

Braga said, "They know we're homeless. Do they know we're from a different time?"

"I don't think so," said Mist Walker. "Unless journeying through time is common to them."

"How do we get back?"

He shrugged. "I'm not sure we can."

"Damn you," she said, "you mean we're stuck in this stinking—"

"When you cut down the Blood Tree, you changed things," he said. "That has to be the explanation. We should've been transported to France. The year should be 1545. But obviously this isn't France and this cannot be the sixteenth century. This must be a city of some far-future time."

"And you can't get us back." She cut her eyes at him.

"I don't know." Mist Walker looked up at the glittering tower above them. "Could be we are meant to be here. This may be no accident."

"Or it may be that Lord Lucifer misdirected us for sport."

A light rain began to fall. The rain did not smell clean and fresh like the rains of Braga's homeland. This rain had an acrid taint that made her nose burn and her eyes water. Even so, it didn't smell as bad as Mulroy, but the stench of rotting flesh didn't bring such tears to her eyes.

Mist Walker was bending over to peer into a green box with a small window. Braga stood beside him and saw that he was reading words on a thick piece of paper behind the strange glass. He read aloud: "'New York Times. September 9, 2013.'"

"Gods," she whispered. "I've heard of York, I think. At least we're in the same part of the world."

"I'm not so sure. But we have to assume that you and Angel Steel have some satanic task to perform here," he said, rubbing the white stubble on his chin, "wherever here is."

"Lucifer *did* send us to this place," she said. "Evil bugger."

Mist Walker smiled and said, "The game is on, then? Are you ready to play it?"

She drew Angel Steel and held it aloft. Lightning flashed overhead. Rain fell harder.

She said, "I am."

"Do you actually think you can beat the Devil?"

The white raven came out of the driving rain and lighted on Mulroy's shoulder. The boy bent down, grabbed a scuttling roach and fed it to the rook.

Braga looked into Krake's beady pink eyes and said, "I don't know, Mist Walker. But I *do* know the Devil cannot beat me. Not so long as I have this sword."

Angel Steel began to glow with a greenish gold light. Braga trembled with pleasure as the sword's power surged into her. Her white hair flared in the wind, her remaining war braid dangling like a live serpent.

When Thomas saw that her eyes glowed with the same green-gold light, he believed she was right.

Nothing could defeat her.

Braga looked deeper into the raven's eyes. With the aid of Angel

Steel's power, she could see the reddish-orange vistas of Hell burning behind Krake's pink orbs. She saw in them as well Lucifer's true face, his subterranean eyes fixed upon her.

"I see you, Devil," she said, showing her teeth in a feral grin. "And I will see that you stay in your place."

Lucifer laughed, and though she couldn't hear his laughter, she felt it as a sickening ripple in the pit of her belly.

She pointed the tip of the sword at the white raven and at the ruler of Hell beyond this strange realm.

Smiling, she said, "The game is on."

XX. SENTINEL

The white raven squawked then took a thin ragged strip of dead flesh from the boy's neck. Mulroy cursed and swatted the big bird off his shoulder.

Braga said, "We have to do something about this damned demon bird. At this rate, the boy will be nothing but sinew and bone in a fortnight."

The raven landed on the green box housing the printed words.

"You're right," said Thomas. "Dead flesh won't heal. I'll try a spell of protection. But I'll need a quiet place. The din of this place is near deafening. That cathedral yonder should do."

Braga looked where Thomas pointed and momentarily lost her breath as she beheld the great size and beauty of the towering structure in the near distance. But she wasn't sure what Thomas meant by his deafening din. The carriages without horses gave off a low growling drone and every now and then a shrill blast from an unseen horn pricked the night air, and there was a constant rumbling hum to this place, as if huge things might be moving at speed beneath the smooth-paved streets and walkways and buildings, but the din was far from deafening. She surmised that Mist Walker's hearing was much more sensitive than her own, though she'd always had sharper hearing than most. For the moment she was more taken with the nighttime lighting of this vast city. Everywhere there were lights but not a single flame. Was this city lit by sorcery?

"Let us go quickly," Thomas said. "I fear we present an odd aspect to the inhabitants of this place. Walk fast and look no one in the eye."

Braga had the sense that they had arrived in the middle of night, partly because there were very few folks moving about on foot. Most of them were inside their wheeled conveyances, behind glass panes. She felt the eyes of some of them briefly lighting on her and her companions but then their carriages hurried them on to whatever destinations awaited them, leaving them to wonder at the odd foreigners they'd just seen. Braga was increasingly confident that no one was interested in stopping them and demanding an accounting of their trespass.

To reach the cathedral they had to cross the stream of carriages. Thomas observed that the flow of traffic seemed to be controlled by the alternately glowing colored discs within yellow boxes suspended over the roadways. "The red stops them, the green makes them go. I can't make out what the yellow one does. When this one goes red again, we can cross over."

They crossed and made their way to the great cathedral. They stood looking up at its soaring arches and daring spires rising heavenward. The sight of such massive majesty left Braga momentarily breathless.

Thomas rested his hands on the crossbeam of his cross-cult staff. "I've heard it said that such a cathedral is a sermon in stone. Now I understand what was meant by it. Can you not see mankind's overpowering desire to exalt Almighty God? To know His unknowable mind?"

"It is...big," she said.

Thomas laughed heartily. "Yes, yes it is, to be sure."

"I'm more taken up with knowing Lucifer's mind and understanding why he moves us through the ages as his game-pieces. If your Almighty wants to intervene or explain why we're here, I'm all ears."

"Perhaps the Lord intends to use you—us—to intervene on His behalf. I have no doubt He wants you to fight against the evil overlord. "

"You were there, in my head," she said. "You spoke to me. You were there in spirit, no?"

"Yes, in a sense. A spell allowed me to find you, to tune to you in a kind of harmony of the spirit. Yes. But I was not truly there as you were. I had no such powerful guide as your renegade angel. I would not be welcome in Hell."

"As I was."

"I speak true when I say to you that your spirit sings at a pitch of ringing power," Thomas said. "You are unique in all the worlds. I am coming to believe that the real battle between good and evil may be fought on the battlefield of your soul. This is why you and I are met. Why Lucifer himself recruited you—or tried to."

Mulroy picked something—an ant's carapace?—out of his nose and flipped it away. The white raven flew after it and caught it in its beak.

"Let's go inside," Thomas said as he lifted his cross and pointed it at the ornate doors of the cathedral.

Something above caught Braga's eye. The stone beast—her mother had once referred to such statues as gargoyles—crouched above a high arch had just stirred. Hadn't it? She stared hard at it, daring it to move once more.

"What is it?" Thomas asked.

"That...gargoyle moved." She put her hand on the hilt of Angel Steel, which was sheathed on her back. She felt the weapon vibrate as if humming silently to itself.

"I doubt stone statues move even in this future world," he said.

"There! You see? Its eyes..."

"Mother of God," Thomas said softly.

The gargoyle's eyes were glowing with a yellowish light. Though it was quite a distance above them, projected from a ledge over an arch, Braga and Thomas both saw the thing's half-folded stone wings slowly fan out and begin to open. A shower of stone dust rained down on them. They brushed grit from their eyes but kept eyes locked on the gargoyle. Mulroy the dead boy cried out as the white raven landed on his shoulder and begin to caw excitedly.

Braga started: "I think the bloody beast's going to—"

Thomas interrupted: "Inside, now!"

But it was too late. The great gargoyle launched itself off its station and swooped straight down at the intruders, its wide span of wings cleaving the air as its huge bear-like paws opened and extended deadly claw-talons.

The dead boy yelped. The raven squawked and went airborne.

Braga drew Angel Steel but before she could properly wield it defensively, the gargoyle was upon them, knocking them *into* the pavement. Miraculously, there was no pain. They should have been crushed but they fell *through* the hard surface. It was like falling through cold water, water that wasn't actually wet. Darkness engulfed them. And still they fell. Angel Steel emitted a soft glow on Braga's right side, her right hand desperately hanging onto its hilt. Likewise, Thomas's cross also began to glow but neither of their lights revealed anything but the darkness swallowing them down.

Falling through ground that had moments before been solid beneath their feet reminded Braga of her descent with the rebel angel into the bowels of the fiery underworld. Had Lucifer sent this stony monster to bring her back to him? No, she didn't think so. Why would he? When it became clear that she was going to survive this fall through the yielding ground, she relaxed and waited for the inevitable confrontation waiting at the end of the fall. If the Lord of the underworld intended that she slay this gargoyle, then so be it. She had no doubt that the angel's sword could make quick work of the beast of living stone.

As they all hit solid ground, the gargoyle spoke in a booming voice: "You will not get past me, hell spawn!"

A purplish light dawned in an eerie sky. The city of the far future was gone, replaced by barren flatlands and distant jagged mountains.

Thomas gained his feet and held his cross aloft but this time it did not burst into flames, nor even glow with otherworldly light in this strange place. "We are not spawn of hell. I follow Jesu. The woman and boy are with me."

"They are fresh from the underworld," the gargoyle said, eyes ablaze. "They wear its stench."

"True enough," Braga said as she stood and brandished the blade, which had not lost its luminescence. "The Lord of Hell seeks to use me for his vile purposes but this sword taken from a dreadful angel makes me strong. And it can easily end you if I will it done."

The gargoyle towered over them on restless feet, thick and cumbersome though they appeared. Its wings had folded so that they were mere ridges on its massive back. "You are not native to my city, nor to its era. Why have you come there?"

"We do not know," she said. "It was not of our choosing. Why have you brought us to *this* place which seems kin to Hell?"

The gargoyle rumbled thoughtfully, then said, "I brought you here to destroy you. This is the place I come to do battle so that I do not have to wreak havoc in the city I am sworn to protect."

Mulroy got to his bare feet. His devilish companion the white raven had not appeared here. Braga wondered if the bird was lost in the between-world darkness. Good riddance if so.

"If you wish to destroy us, then why are we talking?" Braga asked. "Let's get to it and see who gets destroyed."

Thomas stepped between Braga and the gargoyle, holding up his cross. "Wait. Think on it, Braga. Suppose Lucifer sent you to dispatch this creature? Is that what you want? To do his evil bidding? To be so easily used? Have you not sworn to fight the Ruler of Hell, even as he bids you to do his work?"

"It would not be the first time Satan has sent an assassin my way," said the gargoyle. "My own life means little to me, but my sentinel duty is everything. I am sworn to die defending this border."

"Die? I did not know stone could live," Braga said, unable to keep her antagonism in check. Her blood was up and the devastating weapon was charged with godlike energies.

"I was not always this thing of stone. I was flesh and bone, same as you."

The raven burst from the empty air with an eruption of white wings and a startling squawk. The gargoyle swatted the bird to the ground and crushed it beneath a great paw.

"Do not tell me the bird was not hell spawn," the gargoyle said in his tomblike voice.

"Satan's spy," Thomas admitted.

When the gargoyle raised its paw, there was no sign the raven had ever been there.

Dead boy Mulroy allowed a meager smile on his bloodless lips.

A sudden gathering of black flies erased his smile.

Braga kept her eyes on the stone beast. He was huge but she had no doubt Angel Steel could make quick work of him and have off his stones if he had any. But she did not wish to destroy the beast if that was Lucifer's will. She realized that she would need allies to best Lucifer. Now that Lucifer's raven was gone, it was a good time to forge an alliance—if possible.

"Tell me," she said to the gargoyle, "how did the man you were ever agree to become a stone sentinel?"

The gargoyle made a rumbling sound in its wide chest. It blinked its bright eyes and assumed a less threatening posture. Finally he spoke again, this time with a hint of humanity in his inflection. "I will tell you my tale, to forestall combat and perhaps to cleanse my soul. Hear my confession, holy man. But I ask neither forgiveness nor blessing."

Leaning on his cross-cult staff, Thomas nodded assent.

Braga sheathed restless Angel Steel and said, "Get on with it. My patience is thin so see that your tale doesn't plod like ponderous stone."

The gargoyle gave a nod. A ghost of a smile momentarily haunted his large mouth.

Then he told his tale.

XXI. CONFESSIONS OF A GARGOYLE

I was human then. An ordinary man living an ordinary life of meaninglessness. I had determined to kill myself. When the gargoyle spoke to me, I decided to delay my death long enough to hear what more it might have to say. Veiled by swirling tendrils of mist, its monstrous stone face loomed over me, and its cold eyes seemed to hold me in place on the ledge high above the steps of the cathedral.

I had climbed out on the ledge with the intention of hurling myself to my death. I won't burden you with mundane details; I'm sure you've heard it all before. Suffice it to say that life's little skirmishes had beaten me down and that I was ready to jump out of the game altogether.

Up there on the ledge in low-hanging clouds, I was giddy and lightheaded. I was at the edge of existence, balanced precariously on the border between life and death, and the black despair I had known for so long had left me. Once you make the decision to die, you experience immense relief, and everything starts looking a whole lot brighter. At that point you might even begin to believe that you don't need to die after all, that maybe things aren't really *that* bad; but if you try to renege, the despair will come flooding back with a vengeance. I had made that mistake before. I wouldn't make it again. This time I would carry it to conclusion. I would spread my metaphorical wings and fly to my death.

Then the gargoyle spoke.

"Might I have words with you?" it said.

I looked up into the mist-swathed face of stone, saw the wet sheen of its eyes, and I said, "Pardon me?" Hardly a brilliant response. Just one of those inane things humans say to one another in awkward or confusing situations.

The gargoyle said, "It is not within my power to grant pardons."

"Oh," I said. "Well, I wasn't really asking you to."

The gargoyle scowled, I think. It's hard to tell with a gargoyle, since most of them look permanently pissed off.

I saw right away that I had to be very concrete in my comments to the great stone beast. "Yes," I said, "you may have words with me."

"It is well, then," it said. Because the mist was so thick, I wasn't sure if its mouth actually moved when it spoke or if it was using some sort of telepathic communication—or if I'd finally gone completely psychotic.

"You have come here to die. Is this not so?"

"Yes, I have," I admitted. "You are very perceptive."

"A sentinel must be so."

"Ah." Another rather meaningless comment from yours truly. I realized that I wasn't acquitting myself very well as a representative of the human race.

On the street below an ambulance whooped past, its emergency flashers lending the dense fog a red pulse, as though the misty night itself had a visible heartbeat.

"Do you not fear the loss of your soul?" asked the gargoyle.

I pressed my back against the cathedral's mist-slick wall; I didn't want to be blown off the ledge by a random wind. I was determined that the moment of my death would be of my own choosing. "I'm not convinced I have a soul," I said. "I'm not really a religious person. Do you know something I don't?"

"I know you have a soul."

The rising wind dispersed the mist so that I saw that the stone beast's mouth didn't move when it spoke. "Ha! Your mouth didn't move," I said with a hollow laugh. "You're not alive. This conversation is all in my head. Gargoyles don't talk. I'm just a little nuts, is all."

The gargoyle sighed. The sigh sounded like a heavy door of stone rumbling open. "It takes much energy to animate this body of stone. It is not necessary for communication."

I laughed again. "I never knew I had such a vivid imagination. For a minute there I was believing you were actually alive and talking."

"Pay heed," the gargoyle said—commanded.

The wings on its back slowly unfolded, and the creature angled its great head on its thick neck. "Are you satisfied that I am more than a product of your feeble imagination?" This time its mouth moved when it spoke.

"I'm hallucinating," I said, though I wasn't convinced it was so. But what other explanation was there? "If this is real, it's a violation of the laws of physics."

"Your knowledge of such matters is woefully incomplete. Your men of science are only just beginning to glimpse the implications of their so-called quantum physics." His wings were completely unfurled now, the wingspan no less than twenty meters.

"You're a persistent bugger," I said. "I'll give you that."

The gargoyle reached down from its perch and raked a huge talon across my cheek. I cried out in pain and surprise.

"Does a hallucination draw blood?" it asked, the question made rhetorical by its action.

I touched my cheek and felt a warm trickle. Looked at the bloody smear on my fingers. Knew the thing was alive. "Okay," I managed to say. "I...I get it. I see your point."

"It is well." Its wings folded on its back and it withdrew its dragon-like arm from the vicinity of my face. "Such movement is taxing for me in this world."

"You...exist in some *other* world as well?"

"Certainly. Even your less imaginative physicists have learned that certain atomic structures can exist in two places at once. But of course it is all theoretical for them. Abstract mathematics and such."

I was intrigued, hungry to learn more from Old Stone Face. For the first time in months, the spark of curiosity kindled within me. It was as though some psychic pilot light had been relit. "Tell me," I said. "Tell me about this other world."

"Because it suits my purposes, I shall do so. But for you to fully understand, I must take you back hundreds of years to my origin."

"Fine with me," I said. "I've got nowhere to go." *But down*, I thought. "No pressing engagements to keep." *Except for that penciled-in appointment with the Grim Reaper.*

"You have a wry sense of humor. I rather like that."

"Thank you," I said. "You were reading my thoughts, weren't you?"

"Yes. One of my kind sees into the hearts of men. I would be a poor sentinel if I had not that ability."

I sat down on the ledge very carefully, letting my legs dangle in the air. "Well then, let's hear your story, Mr. Gargoyle."

"Very well. And my name is...was Axx, not Mr. Gargoyle."

Properly scolded, I offered humble apologies. Then the gargoyle sketched for me his life story, recounting it with the solemnity of words engraved in stone.

In a time when gods walked the earth and great magic was abroad in the land, I was a simple warrior in the service of a self-crowned king. On a nameless field of battle in Saxony I was struck down by a foeman's blade and lay in the mud, awaiting my final breath. I knew I had been dealt a mortal blow, and that soon the Valkyries would have their "raven's drink" of my blood and bear me to Valhalla. But on that day they did not come as black-feathered Kraken; they came thundering on horseback as fearsome priestess-warriors, Wodan's death angels just the same. They bore me away from the bloody field, across strange moors and into a mist-laden grove of trees. From every tree a rotting corpse hung, and I knew then we were in the sacred grove of Uppsala, where men were sacrificed to the God of the Hanged, the All-father Wodan.

The Valkyries drew up before the largest tree in the grove and tossed me to the ground at the feet of a one-eyed old man with a long gray beard. Leaning on his crooked staff, the old man studied me closely with his one good eye, then laughed, cackling like an old hen. I reached a hand to my breast where I had taken the blow from the blade, but my wound was gone. It came to me then that my body was back on the battlefield, already turning cold in death, and that my spirit-body was intact.

"Why am I here, old man?" I asked, getting to my feet.

He pushed back his black cowl and said, "My pretty angels have brought you to Yggdrasil the gallows tree." He made a gesture with his gnarled hand, and I saw a fresh corpse hanging from the tree of twisted limbs. "Would you put a question to the Hanged Man?"

"A question?"

"The question foremost in your heart." His voice was suddenly very forceful—not at all the voice of a wizened old man.

I blurted out the only question within me. "Why am I not in Valhalla? I fought bravely. I never showed cowardice in battle."

The corpse's eyes opened and his lips began to move. His voice was a ragged whisper, but I heard it clearly enough. "You, warrior, have been chosen to oppose the gods' enemies who would bring on a new Ragnarok. You shall stand guard against those demons who yearn for The Twilight of the Gods and the destruction of the divine order."

Then the Hanged Man fell silent. The one-eyed old wizard raised his staff and said, "Do you accept your fate?"

It was then that I knew that the old man was indeed Wodan, Leader of the Wild Hunt and Conductor of Souls. It was folly to refuse a god, so I gave my assent without hesitation. Thereupon he touched his crooked staff to my head, and my spirit flew from the grove, snatched away like a leaf in a whirlwind. Then I knew absolute stillness. I was engulfed by deepest darkness. Time lost all meaning. Whether I was *locked in that darkness for mere minutes or for interminable eons, I cannot say. I slept the long sleep of the dead, and when at last I awoke, I was as you see me now, inhabiting this body of sculpted stone, perched upon this cathedral as a sentinel.*

In my heart I was still Axx the warrior, but my external shape was that of a great beast. My station was as it is now—at the border of two worlds, the mortal and the immortal. In your realm of mortality, I am a gargoyle, sculpted by a man called Poincarre, but in the netherworld of Immortals, I wear the living flesh of the beast represented by this stone you now see. In the netherworld I do battle with demonic interlopers bent on conquering worlds and usurping the gods.

I and my warrior brothers have fought many bloody battles so that your world may go on. But for us, you would have to face the demons yourselves. Can there be any doubt as to how that would turn out? Ragnarok, my mortal friend. The Twilight of the Gods. What you would call the Apocalypse.

Even now the enemy hordes are massing at the borders of your world. The demonic menace casts its bleak shadow upon the entire earth. Can you not feel its coldness? Would you not like to take part in the great conflict and meet the enemy on the Blooded Plains?

"Me?" I was incredulous. What exactly was the gargoyle proposing? How could I, an insignificant mortal, play a part in this otherworldly war?

"There is a way," Axx answered my unspoken questions. "You were once a warrior yourself, were you not?"

"Well, yes, but it wasn't even a declared war. And I was a draftee, not a volunteer."

"A warrior just the same. You have a warrior's heart, but you live in a time of ambiguity, a time of dubious heroes. I offer you a chance to live or die as a champion of a noble cause. A fate far better than the unsightly suicide you had planned for yourself. But before you decide, you should meet the enemy and taste the combat yourself. Are you game?"

The winds had died and the mist was thicker than before. I could hardly see the gargoyle's face now. An eerie sense of *unreality* was so strong in me that I briefly wondered if I had already jumped to my death and was now in some mystical afterlife wherein the deceased must act out his destined part in a fantastical mystery play. What *was* real for me was the sense of impending adventure—the antithesis of the despair I had harbored for so long. "Yes, I am game."

Without further word, Axx reached down and lifted me off the ledge and set me upon his broad back. Behind me his great wings unfurled to their full width, and we were suddenly airborne, soaring into the unearthly fog. Clinging desperately to his massive neck—no longer stone but flesh—I saw nothing of the familiar skyline of my city, and I sensed that we were already riding the ethereal currents of another realm.

Then we dropped below the clouds and I got my first glimpse of the cratered land of the Blooded Plains. Fires burned in some of the craters, giving the landscape a reddish-orange glow beneath a magenta sky. As we swooped low over the barren ground, Axx said, "You shall see some of the skirmishes preceding the coming battle. There—" he pointed toward a small range of craggy mountains—"is the enemy. Mark him well, for he is a fierce fighter and devourer of souls."

Crouched on a jagged cliff and watching us with evil eye-slits sat a lizard-man with wings. Growing out of each shoulder was a sharp horn curved toward its head, and the leathery membrane of its black wings, at half-mast, were veined in crimson. The demon's reptilian skin glowed with the swirling coloration of a New World coral snake. It opened its fang-filled mouth and emitted a shrill screech that was undoubtedly a war cry, then the beast took to the air, flying up to meet us in combat.

The gargoyle had the advantage of being twice as big as the demon, but the demon was swifter and more agile. It flew shrinking rings around us, and I knew it was looking for an opening, seeking just the right moment to strike.

"Hold tight," Axx told me, though he needn't have; I was holding on for all I was worth.

Then the demon darted in for the strike. The attack came from above and behind us, and I realized the lizard-man's intention was to snatch me from the gargoyle's back. Beyond that, I didn't know what it had planned for me (Rip me apart? Drop me to the ground?), but I knew it couldn't be healthy. I feared that it saw me as a tender and tasty morsel for a mid-battle snack.

But Axx had anticipated the demon's tactic, and with uncanny quickness, the gargoyle swatted the demon with a powerful whipping motion of his tail. There was a resounding *pop* like the snap of a gigantic bullwhip, and I craned my head to see the demon, its wings collapsed, hurtling to the ground.

Axx didn't hover about to see the demon's fatal impact with the orange earth. Instead, he flapped his wings and powered us onward, over mountainous crags, then down close to the ground where other gargoylish creatures were engaged in death matches with wingless demons.

"Have you seen enough?" Axx asked.

Seeing a swarm of demons bring down a griffon-like gargoyle, I shouted into the wind, "Yes, thank you." We rose up through amethyst clouds, hurtled through otherworldly mists, and within minutes, I was back on the ledge overlooking the cathedral steps and Axx was once again at his stony station.

"So you have seen the Blooded Plains and the Sawtooth Mountains," Axx observed. "Did your blood not stir with battle-lust? Would you not like to enter the fray as a noble warrior?"

"It was certainly...exciting," I said. "But how would I...Would I have to be like you? I mean, how does a man become a gargoyle?"

"You and I would simply trade places. You would inhabit this body, and I yours."

"You would be me?"

"In body only. You would maintain the integrity of your soul."

"And you would no longer be a...what you are."

"That is so. My soul is very old. I have grown weary of the fight," he explained. "I no longer have the heart for it. You, on the other hand, are a young soul with a youthful warrior's heart."

I suddenly became very suspicious. Was Axx trying to pull a fast one?

He said, "I must confess the true inclination of my heart. I am in love."

"*What*? You? In love?" I tried not to laugh.

"Aye, deeply. A woman who comes daily to the cathedral to light a candle for her dead husband has captured my heart. She has such purity of soul as I cannot describe to you. She reminds me of the wife I had long ago, when I too was a man. It may even be that she *was* my wife in that other lifetime. I am not yet certain."

"So your stony old heart has been softened by a woman. Who'd have thought it?"

"It is so. Then the Fates brought you here, and now my heart leaps in exhilaration at the thought of being with her as a mortal. Would you who were ready to throw your life away deny me a chance to court the woman I love?"

"But I would be trapped within that…that hideous body of stone. No offense."

"If you wished to end your tenure as a sentinel, you could let the demons slay you on the Blooded Plains."

"And my soul? What would happen to it? You said the demons devour souls."

"The souls of mere men, yes. But the soul of a sentinel would be freed to return to the Great Wheel, from whence you would likely be spun off in a new incarnation."

I was overwhelmed, to say the least. But more than that, I was intrigued by the improbable possibilities. I was being offered a rare opportunity, an alternative to futile self-destruction. A reason to go on living had been set before me, and all I had to do was embrace it. A strange new life of noble adventure beckoned, yet I hesitated. "I'll need some time to think it over," I said after a long silence.

"Certainly," Axx agreed. "While the passage of time is of little consequence to me, it takes its toll on the woman who unwittingly holds my heart in her thrall. I pray you find the wisdom to make your decision without undue delay."

In truth, I needed no time to think the matter over. My course was set. My decision made. As you see me now, I am what I am. Old Axx is walking around in my traded-in body, happy as the proverbial lark, and I am the sentinel, sworn to eternal duty.

XXII. OLD GODS SLEEPING, DEVIL SHIP RISING

Braga said, "Eternity is long. Stone crumbles over time."

"This is so," the gargoyle said. "But stone is not my true nature. I am as you see me, here. Back in the other world I wear the heavy mantle of stone, suitably disguised from those without the secret knowledge."

Braga addressed Thomas: "These tales within tales make me weary. By all the gods, I wonder if I am not back on Hag Mountain, drunk from the sap of the sacred tree of bloody knowledge."

Thomas said, "The old gods sleep the sleep of the dead. The one true God may guide us if we keep our eyes open. You know the sentinel speaks true?"

"Yes. And I have no wish to wake these old gods. Tell us, gargoyle, why have you not told us your name? When you were a man, did you come from the city where we found you? Or like us, did you come from a far-off time?"

"My name is unimportant. I have no use for it. I was of the time and place of the city where you found me. An older time, I think, than yours. By which I mean a future far from your place and time of origin." Something like a smile played over the gargoyle's giant protruding teeth. "You are wise to let sleeping gods lie. Some of them are very light sleepers."

Braga sheathed Angel Steel. "You brought us here, Nameless. Will you get us away from this forsaken place between worlds? Or must we wait for Lucifer's evil hand to move us to the next damned location?"

"Because I believe you are what you say you are, I will return you, though you will be out of place there, given your manner of dress and weaponry. No one carries a sword there."

"No one anywhere carries a sword such as this one," she said. "Stolen from a renegade angel amid the fires of Hell."

The gargoyle dipped his big head. "As you say. Then had we fought, I would've died here this day."

"Most certainly. Unless you are more cunning than you look and a great deal faster. So this hellish place is where you fought the demons you told of in your story?"

"One of several such places I have fought, though I reckon they are joined by the same underworld. Look closely at the rocky ground and sandy pits and you will find buried bones and scattered pieces of the desiccated corpses of fallen warriors and various demons."

"Boy? What are you doing?" Thomas asked Mulroy, who had dropped to his knees to shovel a handful of dirt into his mouth, then another. The boy said nothing. He had uttered few words since they had been catapulted from Hell.

Thomas looked at Braga. Braga shrugged. "He's a living corpse," she said. "He has no need of food. Perhaps the dead crave dirt?"

The ground trembled. Mulroy spat out a mouthful of reddish sandy dirt, his eyes gone huge with their whites.

"Something is coming," the gargoyle said. "You may get to use that Heaven Sword yet."

"Bugger," she said, echoing the favored curse of her lost clan.

Thomas said a prayer and the cross atop his staff began to glow an eerie green. Braga had not seen it green before and wondered if it was taking its color from the strange land they stood upon. If so, would Mist Walker's prayers be any good here? Or would they, too, be tainted and tinted by the hellish landscape?

The ground trembled with stronger ferocity. Mulroy was on all fours now, spitting bits of dirt from his tongue. The gargoyle ambled forward several steps and planted his big legs as if bracing for immediate attack.

"What comes?" Braga shouted above the deep rumble coming from under the ground.

"Nothing good," the gargoyle answered with a shake of his great head.

The ground split open and from a narrow fissure of showering sand the white raven flew from it, wings shining as if white-hot from the fires of the underworld.

"The old gods may be sleeping but the devil sends his minions," the gargoyle growled. Then he stamped his forefeet in a war dance that might've been comical in different circumstances.

Braga drew Angel Steel. Mulroy's fingers came out of the dirt with a tarnished short sword as if the dirt he'd eaten had whispered to his innards of the lost blade's existence. A grimacing smile split his young, dead face. Thomas mouthed a monotone a prayer to the mother of Jesu and his cross shone brighter.

The raven attempted to land on the dead boy's shoulder, probably for yet another bite of carrion flesh, but Mulroy struck its head off with his newfound short sword and the raven's beak tasted only dirt while its headless body twitched on the ground before finally going legs-up and stiff.

"Well done, boy," Braga said. "Lucifer won't be happy with that."

In the lowland depression before them a pattern began to draw itself in the red sand, an outline, a shape Braga was quick to recognize: the shape of a seagoing vessel. Moments later it was more than an outline. An actual ship was surfacing in the shifting sands.

"Bugger," she said, mostly to herself, because it felt good blowing off of her lips and tongue. But also because she felt fear. Felt it down to her bones, head to toe. But then she remembered the powerful weapon in her strong grasp and the blade began to glow again, as if heating up for battle with a warship of the dead—or worse.

The masts of the ship were rigged with no sails. An angry wolf's head rode the vessel's tall prow, its mouth wide and fixed with over-sized fangs, ferocious eyes glaring from its skull. As more of the ship came up, it was plain to see that the vessel was a skeleton ship. Only a frame of a ship, one never meant to be seaworthy.

"A burial ship," Thomas said, echoing Braga's exact thought. Though she had never seen one for herself, she had heard that raiders from the northern seas sometimes buried their chieftains in such as this skeletal vessel rising from the ground. How else were they supposed to make it under sail to the afterlife? Such a voyage to the underworld might take a long time and so the ship was loaded with all the material goods a soul would need for the dark trip.

But as it surfaced, it became clear that this particular burial ship was crewed by undead warriors ready to fight.

"A warship, more like," Braga said, looking hard into the decayed faces of the ship's crew of corpses standing ready to jump overboard with rusted blades of battleaxes and swords, spears and pikes. A few of the undead had hammers that looked heavy enough for Thor himself. "How is that ship even moving?"

"Winds from Hell need no sails to move a devil ship. Satan is not pleased that you refused to slay the gargoyle. Now he wants his revenge."

Braga raised her blade. "Then let him try to take it."

The small sea of red sand caught fire, flames erupting from roiling grains and grit. The ship of the dead rode the flames as a vessel rides rolling swells of the sea. The fire blackened the ship's ribs but did not burn them.

Then Braga heard the sound she never expected to hear again. Her dead mother's womb-song, the song that had found her ears to foretell of her mother's death. How could this be?

And yet there she was. Braga's mother, tied to the long neck of the warship, lashed just beneath the carved head of the fierce wolf. She was naked, her breasts no longer the proud paps they had once been, but nevertheless buoyed by the thick rope beneath them that held her fast to the skeleton ship. Her mouth wide with her haunting song.

"Do you see her?" Braga asked Thomas. "The old woman bound to the boat?"

"I do. But these sights aren't to be trusted. Lucifer is Lord of Lies and this is his Hell ship."

"She's my mother. Dead though she surely is."

"Ignore her. Use the sword. The demons are almost upon us and the fire feels real enough. I have no doubt that it will burn our flesh."

The crew of ghouls beat their fiery swords on smoking shields and moaned and wailed their undead chant. The sound was so eerie that chills broke out on her arms and on the back of her neck, in spite of the brutal heat from the Devil's sea of burning sand.

The thing that looked the spitting image of Braga's mother sang louder. The song reached into Braga's belly and wrenched her innards. Undeterred, she gripped Angel Steel with both hands, held it high and felt its otherworldly current flowing through it and through her arms and shoulders, through her breasts and belly, down to her feet. The soles of her feet grew so hot that she almost danced to shake off the burning pain.

When the skeleton ship was almost upon them, she twisted her wrists and slowly swung the mighty sword, bringing its point to bear upon the ship and its demon crew. A bright line of light shot from the sword's point and cut a path through the reddish smoke to the vessel of the dead and damned. The beam of heavenly light sliced through the ship and the ship collapsed upon itself.

Braga did not hesitate, though her light beam also cut her singing mother in half, the old woman's hips and legs falling away into the flames below.

Thomas held his cross higher and it glowed with such intensity that he had to squint his eyes nearly shut, then it dimmed as the ship of the dead sank into the flaming sand and was gone. The fires flickered out.

"Praise God!" Thomas shouted. "We did it."

"We?" Braga gave Angel Steel a shake as its long line of devastating light seemed to retract into the tip of the glowing blade.

"Don't make the mistake of thinking we defeated Satan's minions without the aid of Heaven."

"I beat them with a weapon stolen from a renegade angel of your Lord. I give you that and that is all I can give. What say, gargoyle?"

The gargoyle thundered with laughter. "I'm glad you and your sword are on the right side of things. I've survived many wounds from demons, but I could not have lived against your lost sword of Heaven."

She sheathed it. "Well, can you get us out of this place now? I do not like its look, nor smoky stench."

A new white raven materialized amid the flutter and flap of its wings. The dead boy scowled and threatened the bird with his new-found short sword and the creature wisely kept its distance, cawing three times in complaint. Krake apparently had many lives to yield.

"Yes, I can take you from here. Climb on my back and we'll fly back to the civilized world."

"We have no place in that world," Braga said. "Can you not get us back to our own time?"

"I don't know your time. Nor do I wish to. And anyway, it's beyond my power to do so. Consult those that brought you."

"I couldn't find my way back into Hell even if I wanted to—which I do not," she told him as she climbed onto his broad shoulders, above his folded wings. She motioned to the dead boy and Mulroy gave her his hand and she pulled him up to sit between her thighs. Thomas used his holy staff for leverage and braced it on the ground so he could walk up the gargoyle's side as if climbing a small mountain. He sat directly behind Braga, holding his cross-topped staff high.

"Hold tight," the gargoyle said then spread his great wings, ran and jumped, and off they flew into the purple murk.

A long and frightening moment later, they found themselves dumped in a human pile on the smooth hard surface in front of the great cathedral, looking up at the blur that became the gargoyle perched on his ledge, stone once again, to all appearances. They quickly stood, brushing themselves off, failing to shake the feeling of embarrassment at having been so unceremoniously dumped back in this noisy, terrifying city of the future.

"Now what?" Braga asked no one in particular.

As if in answer, a young man astraddle a strange mechanical contraption with two skinny black wheels came around the corner, speeding silently toward them. His legs were bare and he wore a cap whose shape made Braga think of a duck's bill. The young man's legs were muscular and he worked them up and down, apparently to make his wheels go. A white raven gave aerial escort to the lad on wheels, gliding just above his head.

"Message for you," the young man said after he halted his machine in front of Braga and her two companions. The raven landed on the machine's steel handles.

"Message from Lucifer, no doubt," Thomas said.

"Well, let's have it then," Braga snapped at the lad.

The young man's eyes glowed like hot coals as he said, "Follow the raven."

Mulroy grunted and shook his short sword at this new bird.

"That's it? That's the message?" Braga said, frowning severely. "Follow this Hell bird?"

The messenger smiled, showing long and dangerous teeth. "That's it." Then he pushed off and rode away, bare legs pumping hard to build speed. The white raven flew off and trailed the messenger a moment before looping back to land at Braga's feet. She resisted the impulse to kick the creature as hard as she could.

She looked at Thomas. "How are we to follow a damned bird?"

"We cannot," he said, "unless the foul creature wishes it so. And seeing as how Lucifer is calling the tune, it will wish us to follow."

"And if we lose it or kill it, the Devil will send another." She watched as the raven landed on the dead boy's shoulder, Mulroy slapping at it, missing. "Lead on, you feathered fiend. I want to be quit of this stinking place."

"Whether it's part of my visions not yet revealed to me," said Thomas, "or some other hint from Jesu, I feel as though Lucifer and God are once again battling one another. This time, however, they are using us in some sort of time-warped chess match, and they are battling with our lives."

"Pray your God is better at chess," replied Braga almost as an order.

The raven led them, flying up and swooping low to make it easier for groundlings to keep up with it. The immense structures with countless windows of glass towered over them like canyons through which they trekked in pursuit of Hell's white raven. For all its threatening size and intimidating vehicles of conveyance, the city did possess an otherworldly beauty, exotic and somehow intoxicating. There was a powerful inevitability here, one she trusted due to her communion with the Blood Tree on Hag Mountain.

They followed the raven round corners and along byways, some crowded with strangely dressed people who doubtless thought Braga and her two companions clownishly dressed. More than a few folk looked with naked alarm at the sword she wore on her back, its beautiful handle riding above her right shoulder leaving little doubt that she bore on her back an instrument of quick death and destruction. None of these city dwellers wore swords, nor arms of any sort that she could see. Except for the single horseman now riding toward them along the street, a man dressed in a dark blue uniform of strange cut and a shiny round helmet, with a small cudgel on one hip and a small weapon holstered in leather on his other hip. Though Braga had never seen a weapon of such shape and size, something in the way the man sat on his horse told her that it was a formidable weapon and that he rode with a certain official authority.

"This looks like trouble," she said under her breath.

The horseman came on, his eyes taking in what he obviously saw as a curious spectacle of oddly attired strangers escorted by a huge white raven. He reined his mount to a halt, looked down at them and said, "Nice outfits," he said. "Where's the party?"

The horseman's language was not easy to understand and if Braga hadn't sipped the sap of the Blood Tree, she probably could not have understood a word. Rather than verbalize an answer, she merely nodded in the direction ahead.

"That a real sword?" the horseman asked.

"Yes," she answered.

"I could charge you with carrying a menacing weapon but that getup you're wearing makes you anything but. If you're going to join the occupiers, you'd best not take that big blade. Some of those folks might think you were looking for dragons to slay and try following you to Hobbit Land or something." The horseman chuckled. "Or steal it right off your back."

Braga didn't know what he was talking about, but she laughed at his obvious attempt at humor.

A new sound rose above the droning din of this city: drumbeats. Distant but most certainly there nonetheless. A series of sharp reports overrode the drumbeats, and the horseman turned his mount and rode off at a gallop in the direction of the echoing din.

The white raven led them by short lazy flights through the acrid air and between tall buildings of boring design. Finally, they came to a dark-stoned structure of moderate height with a glowing sign above its entrance: HOTEL AMERICANA GRAND. The first letter of each word was red, the other letters blue, so that if you read just the red letters they spelled: H A G.

Thomas put what she was thinking in words: "This could well be this city's Hag Mountain. A jump-off to other worlds."

It did possess a sinister look about it, and the way the lights glowing from its many windows and the lighted sign revealed tendrils of mist about the place, even though nearby structures didn't appear to be mist-ringed.

A banshee wail shrilled and trilled somewhere in the strangely-lit night.

A long, tall carriage pulled up in the front of the HAG. Braga caught herself reading the big letters on the side of its metal carapace: Second-Sight Seers' Tour. She said, "Since I drank of that bloody tree I notice that I can read any language, even though I don't even know what bloody language it is I'm reading."

The carriage disgorged a gaggle of passengers of various races, speaking different languages. Braga understood every word she heard. "And I can hear and understand them all as well."

Thomas nodded. "There will be many things you'll be surprised to learn that you know, not all of them things you will wish to know."

"I know too bloody much already. There goes the damned bird into the place. Let's follow the bugger. And move quickly. This odd band of folk may be going in this place, too, and we should avoid the crush."

Follow they did. Up a stairway to the ninth floor. The white raven landed in front of the door to room 909. Braga, Thomas and Mulroy all stood as if frozen while the raven shat on the carpet, then flew off down the long dim corridor and disappeared in shadow. Thomas rapped on the door and tried the doorknob. It turned. The door swung open. The stench of death hit them full force.

A corpse sat slumped in a chair at a cluttered desk.

"Gods," Braga said. "What's this, a joke?"

Then the corpse opened his mouth and said, "Fresh from hell you are. Lord Lucifer sends his regards."

"A living corpse," Braga said with distaste. This heap of talking rot was more putrid than Mulroy. The boy's decay seemed to have all but ceased—no doubt halted by the Ruler of Hell's evil influence. "Satan sent us here for this obscenity?"

The corpse-man smiled—at least Braga thought it was a smile. The skin around the mouth and eyes cracked and a piece of desiccated flesh fell off.

"I am more than a living corpse," the thing said in a voice at once dry and sodden. "I am Demoriel, Beloved of God. My name is legend in some parts."

Thomas made the sign of the cross, then said, "Dispatch him now and be done with this abomination."

Mulroy looked worriedly at his elder brother of living death.

Braga sat on the edge of a disheveled bed and said, "No. Let's hear his tale. I will not act too hastily in forced service to the Devil. If there is a way to thwart him, I will find it, even if it's only to tweak his evil nose. We should know the lay of the landscape before we go leaping into an abyss."

Thomas nodded, scowled. "But this is a dangerous place. I sense… presences. We should not tarry here long."

Braga clasped her hands in front of her and said, "Tell us your story, Demoriel, Beloved of God. We are all ears and remembering."

XXIII. THE SEVENTH DEMON'S TALE

We were seven when *he* drove us out and left within me this wound that never heals, a raw lesion as foreign to me as a ruthless conscience. I was the first in her and the last to leave, which may explain why the other six were not so devastated. It was a territorial thing, I admit. Perhaps I was too prideful. She was *mine* and I wasn't leaving without a fight. I wish now that we'd been harder on her before *he* evicted us. We should've made her grovel longer, deeper in filth. We should've marred her flesh with lifelong scars. Would that we had been more assiduous in sullying her soul before he came along and crippled me for eternity.

His touch changed me in ways too humiliating to say. He *knew* me. He called me by name, and now I am become something other than what I was—a thing I hardly recognize. I am a deviant shunned by my own kind, mocked openly in the Lower Quarter. My name has become synonymous with *fool*. Demoriel, Beloved of God, they call me, delighting in the derision. I am the butt of mock tributes and comic atrocities throughout the low-order grottoes and far-flung archipelagos in the Great Sea of Darkness.

The song of my shame sizzles even in the dreary patter of sleet on mortals' panes. All because *he* touched me when *he* drove me out of that insufferable woman from Magdala. The other six growled and grumbled but wisely took their leave without undue delay. Naamah the Seducer, Rimmon the Syrian Devil, Zaebos the Count of Hell, Veltis the Scourge of Babylon, Thamuz the Summerian Braggart (who now claims he invented artillery *and* started the Inquisition) and Noxious Nergal of the Second Order—not one of them suffered the torment wrought within me by Yeshua, nor the ridicule that followed—and follows me still.

I suffered deeply down the dark ages, a virtual outcast, forced to walk the cutting edges of the worlds, not belonging in any of them. A creature of darkness with a shameful lust for the Light. I, who corrupted the bodies and souls of countless pathetic mortals, no longer able to do spiritual violence? No wonder I was mocked and scorned.

I was attired in the sallow flesh of a gray-haired monk when the summons from Satanael reached me. Croucher by the Door delivered it. It has been rumored that Croucher was one of the seven in partial possession of Miriam's soul, but this hearsay only serves to illustrate how little the human world knows of our kind. A demon of Croucher's rank is never allowed to touch a mortal. Croucher is what you might call an inner-circle "flunky." He crouches by the door to the Dread Lord's chamber, always at the Son of the Morning Star's beck and call. While his physiognomic maladies do make him seem the stuff of mortal nightmares, no human has eyes sensitive enough to see him. When he passes, you might feel a nasty chill or briefly choke on an offensive odor of mysterious origin, but you could never catch even the most fleeting glimpse of him.

Croucher came out of the darkness gathered in the corner of the monk's cell. The pious brother was seated on his prayer mat, trying to reconcile the ravages of the Black Death with God's mercy—with little success. He was aware of me only as a vague disquiet that often interfered with his deeper meditations, and I had no intention of giving away my presence. My purpose was finding a way to the Light, not devastating the monk's soul. I wore him like a roomy habit, well concealed within the flaccid folds of his flesh. I was there as an observer. A seeker. Croucher was oblivious to such nuance of purpose. He came forth as a single-minded shadow to whisper the summons and then dissolved back into darkness.

Lord Satanael would see me at my earliest convenience. One did not ignore such a directive—unless one desires to spend the rest of one's interminable existence chained to tedious chores in the deepest trench of the Lower Quarter, with no possibility of reprieve.

The summons gave me the impetus I needed to depart the monk; for all his spiritual yearning and dedication, the fellow was a dullard. His meditations were often spoilt by thoughts of his next bowl of gruel or the next slice of warm bread. Cohabitation with him was not going to draw me nearer to the Light.

I should explain: I am in no way mortal, nor will I ever become so. It is not the human fear of death that makes me burn for the Light. My kind seldom dies. We may devolve into something resembling a large warty toad, a humpbacked homunculus or a mindless blob of protoplasmic goo, but death almost never claims us. When the Son of the Light reached into Magdalene to force me out, *he* touched me, ignited something in me with *his* power—something still smoldering which threatens to flare brighter than a storm on the sun. None of this is to say I am not on intimate terms with death. I know death inside out. As you see, I'm in the body of a dead man at this very moment, and I have been using his fingers to set down this story I'm now telling you, though the blackened digits go mushy against the lettered keys and the flesh is sloughing off. Damnation, eh?

But I am getting ahead of myself. I've inhabited human flesh so often that I have adopted, more or less, a linear sense of time, but sometimes—such as now—my native perception of time intrudes and I want to leap about, moving forward or backward at will, and in confusing fashion.

But back to the summons. I wasted no time in departing the monk. Leaving him to his quotidian search for the Light in a bowl of gruel, I slid out of him as discreetly as a silent fart escapes a matron's rectum in a front-row pew. In fact, he did fart at the exact instant I exited—and such a fragrant fanfare it was!

I translated myself immediately to the Lower Quarter, not pausing (as I used to do before my feverish affliction) to admire the asymmetries of the Dark Sea's shoreline where it encroaches upon the human realm. I had never had an audience with Satanael and I didn't want one now. I drifted down the dim corridor to the great iron door to the Dread Lord's chamber. I rapped and waited. For the Son of Dawn "brought down to the grave," as some pious Hebrew scribe once wrote of him.

Finally, the great door opened with a groan and Lilith appeared in the annoying splendor of seductress. During this era Lilith was a fixture at the Lower Palaces, privy to court secrets and intrigues. No arse was kissed nor diddled without her knowing every mundane detail, no nefarious plot hatched outside of her hearing—or that of her proxies, her bottom-feeding parasitic spies.

"Demoriel," she said, her long tongue lashing voluptuous lips. "Beloved of—"

"Don't say it," I said. "Don't say *his* name."

Lilith laughed. Her laughter spawned legions of slithering echoes. I wanted to do great violence to her. Delighted to defy me, she said God's Secret Name, long forbidden here. I cringed and gnashed my long teeth.

Lilith reached between my loins to fondle me. Her lust for my kind was legendary, but I knew this fondling was mere mockery because she knew I had been corrupted by the Light and had lost much of the daemoniac fury that could inflame her prodigious carnal appetites.

I seized her wrist and said, "I am summoned by the Dread Lord."

"As I was summoned by God's angels and commanded to mate with Adam, and you know how *that* turned out."

"You refused and proceeded to fuck every earthbound demon you could find."

Lilith shrugged, her breasts writhing restlessly within her leather bodice; in the World Next Door a volcano rumbled, convulsed and belched smoke. "Adam favored fucking his sheep anyway, so that simple cunt Eve was the perfect mate for him. He could never have survived me. And he certainly would not have satisfied me."

"Stand aside," I said.

"I wouldn't go in there if I were you."

I pushed her aside and entered the chamber.

Satanael greeted me with much warmth—too much warmth. I bowed and kept what I hoped was a safe distance. Three walls of his great chamber were living murals reflecting red-tinted scenes of Heavenly beings; by what magic Morning Star animated these scenes, I had no idea. The fourth wall was studded with countless trophy heads of dead mortals, the faces of which were similarly animated with grimacing contortions. A number of them appeared to be mouthing soundless words, pleading, while others were silently screaming.

"We have watched you with great interest," Satanael said, "since your encounter with the Magician."

"With the Son of—"

"We call him Magician for all his pedestrian tricks."

The great mural on the left wall dissolved into a muddle of colors, which then resolved itself into sharp focus as a writhing orgy of Egyptian gods, some with heads of hideous beasts, others with human heads. The angels in the other two murals were compelled to witness the varieties of carnal perversions and ingenious couplings, triplings, and in a few cases, quadruplings.

"As you no longer serve your nature," said Satanael, "I have brought you here to charge you with one last chance to extinguish your unnatural desire for the Light."

The enormous head of his phallus peeked out from the golden folds of his magnificent robe. I knew then that the rumors were true: Satanael's phallus had grown larger in proportion to his aeons spent away from God's light, and in the fertile darkness of his dominion it wasn't done growing. This erotic ratio was fearsome even to me.

"You will receive two gifts," he went on, "to symbolize the battle raging within you. This is the Magician's foreskin, circumcised in the usual tribal ritual and fashioned into this ring. You will henceforth wear it on your little finger as a symbol of your lust for *him*."

He slid the leathery ring onto my finger. Then he grabbed me, spun me round, bent me over and rammed that huge phallus up my arse. "And I give you the gift of my seed to put iron in your withered wick!"

The mural angels turned away in horror. The Egyptian gods looked on in envy. I screamed as his semen flooded into me and inflamed my innards. Lilith howled in laughing delight.

The Dread Lord pushed me away and it felt as if his phallus had pulled my guts out. Lilith took my hand and led me out. I didn't like the way she was looking at me, but the pain in my anus absorbed the lion's share of my attention.

Lilith took me down to the bank of the River of Fire and rode my engorged cock until it was raw and bloodied. When at last she fell off me and sank, sated, into soft ground, I stumbled to my feet and went on my dreary way—the way pointed out to me by my raging phallus.

I proceeded to cut a swath through humanity that became legendary. I laid souls to waste where I found them, allotting no time to look for the Light. I was quick and brutal, working without the subtleties I'd always savored. Centuries passed but I did not lose my desire for the Light. (Yes, even then I reckoned time by the Christian calendar.) No atrocity was great enough to extinguish the flame of desire that still burned within me. I took little pleasure in my work. The evil seeds I sowed in the human race yielded no joy for me. By the 1800's most of my devilish rage was gone, and I went once again in search of the Light.

As I could not take possession of the virtuous souls of saints and true holy men, I went after artists and poets. Anyone who opened himself, either deliberately or whimsically, to unseen influences was fair game, and I the cunning muse. I confess that I took some small pride in directing the creative urges of men like Baudelaire, Poe and Van Gogh, though it did cost them dearly. I had much in common with them. They hungered as did I for the ineffable, for a measure of grace, for a portion of Pure Light or mystical enLightenment. I take no credit for their talents, having only provided daemonic inspiration for their darker works. But in the end, my labors with them brought me no closer to the divine luminescence I'd glimpsed in Yeshua. So I withdrew for a time from all men and attached myself to the underside of the mortal world and sank into solitude.

Then came my mad nun. Perhaps I heard her deranged yet impassioned prayers because my finger bore the ringed foreskin of the

Son of Light: I was, in a sense, a "bride" of Christ, too. Whatever the reason, I entered her with ease and immediately felt at home there. Perhaps you have seen a grove of small trees growing near the seashore and have marveled at the way the brisk sea breezes have permanently twisted their limbs into bizarre reaching postures. The young nun's soul was similarly twisted by the winds of her dementia, reaching ever outward in spiritual desperation. Her warped interior was precisely the environment I needed at the time. I settled in and promptly fell in love with her.

Now I must tell you a secret. A secret that even the most experienced exorcists know nothing about. I hinted at it when I told you the Evil One buggered me. Though it is against my nature to reveal such things, there is no other way for you to understand my unholy union with the nun. One of my kind needs nourishment to thrive. We feed on the darker impulses and overwhelming anguish of those we inhabit; we feast on mortal dread, doubt and fear, and then we loose the foulest excrement into the pits of their souls, which in turn increases their vile emotions and makes for an even richer repast. This evil cycle continues until the host dies or until its soul is so devastated that it no longer offers a viable abode. In this way I ate and shat my way through many a mortal soul.

But with this nun it was different. I didn't occupy her to foul the seat of her soul. I did it in hopes of finding a way to the Light; instead, I found love. Need I say it? A demon knows little of love and isn't meant to be capable of experiencing it directly. And yet I found it in the heart and twisted soul of my demented little nun. Once I'd made myself at home inside her, we spent many an idle hour gazing into a secret looking-glass at our reflection.

Unlike angels, we demons cannot fully materialize in the mortal world—which is precisely why we must take possession of human vessels in order to do our work. Nevertheless, I could see the reflection of my presence in her face and in her glowing eyes. She was looking for the divine spark within herself and I was doing my best to help her find it. The intensity of her desire to know her Savior was too much for her small heart to contain, and deeper madness was inevitable. I zealously wallowed in her mad love, hoping my little nun would find the Magician in the extremities of her religious mania.

She did not. But her search made me realize what I had been after since my fateful encounter with *him*. It was at the heart of my longing for the Light. I wanted to be *saved*. Ridiculous, no? A preposterous weakness in a daemonic being. A perversion of absurd proportion. Beyond ironic. Unthinkable!

When angels assembled around her bed I knew I would have to leave her. I was in no condition to challenge them, so I left her masturbating with a candlestick, my farewell gesture to her and to her greedy guardians.

After the nun, I took possession of a series of ambitious radio and TV preachers. They were all charlatans so it was easy to set up housekeeping in them. My plan was to deceive those pious sinners into thinking I was an angel sent to lead them to salvation. It's a standard tactic for a demon to disguise himself as an inner angelic voice in order to misguide the human host, but my goal was not to lead them to the Sea of Darkness. I wanted to set them on the path to the Light. With only one of them did I come close to reaching the goal, but in the end the evangelical's "conversion" crumbled when he exposed himself to his tent congregation and began to flog his phallus in front of the mortified crowd. Mortals often respond to daemonic presence in such unforeseen ways. I left him as he was preparing to hang himself with his belt.

I kept to myself for a long spell, avoiding the low places where a new summons from Satanael might too easily find me. I took refuge in a small country church in a no-name hamlet and went to sleep in the bigger-than-life crucifix behind the altar. Carved wood makes a good resting place, though it promotes tumultuous dreams. Most demons prefer the dreamless slumber an idol of cold stone offers, but I craved the porous warmth of wood fashioned in the likeness of the Son of Light. I clung to the silly notion that the prayers of *his* worshipers might afford me a measure of divine protection.

When the dreams came, they terrified me. They came up from the earth and down from the stars. They came from the living and as well as the dead. I became a teeming conduit of cosmic nightmares and numinous desires. The sacred and the profane commingled as they coursed through me and streamed out into chaos. I stood my ground and maintained the iconic posture on the cross, fully prepared to sacrifice myself to the greater glory of the God of Light.

I knew I'd failed when Satanael buggered Christ in my dream.

I fled in the decrepit vessel of a repentant warrior, an elderly man who'd knelt at the altar to pray for forgiveness for killing civilians in wartime. Surprisingly, he was acutely aware of my presence and believed I was an invisible instrument of God sent to purify his soul with torment. I chose not to disabuse him of that belief. Moreover, I wondered if I might serve the Light in just such a manner. A tiger can't change his stripes, but he can be sufficiently tamed to serve his master.

I made the old soldier my test case, my lab rat. I thought that if I administered just enough psychic punishment, I could cleanse him of his past sins; I would serve the Light by preparing his soul for ascension. If it worked, I reasoned, then my good deed should attract the attention of heavenly powers and my sincerity would be recognized. But in the end, the old soldier's soul was too frail to withstand even my restrained ministrations and he fell back into his murderous habits and went on a rampage with a high-powered rifle. He gunned down six innocents before the police felled him with a headshot.

I would have to find some other way of getting the attention of the Son of Light.

Wandering once again between worlds, I began a descent into a madness of my own. Were I not mad, I wouldn't be writing this down like a dutiful scribe, or talking to you, revealing forbidden secrets. But I had faith, faith that the gates of madness might open to salvation. In exhilarating desperation, I decided to take a lesson from legendary Lazarus.

I would make the dead walk.

Never mind that reanimated Lazarus never lost the stench of the grave and dreamed every night of maggots eating his flesh.

I would make the dead walk.

It's a trick nearly as old as humanity. A demon has the ability to extend the life of his host in order to prolong the demoniac's suffering. The mortal's soul can even be made to remain for a time in its decaying body, which is on a sort of daemonic life-support. The soul's suffering is exquisite, but the risk to the demon is grave. Stay too long and you become imprisoned in mortal flesh until it turns to waxy stew, or even to dust. The trick is to depart at just the right moment before the rancid flesh slams shut on you, leaving the human's soul to shrivel.

I invaded the soul of a dying hermit sunk in the mire of a spiritual crisis. Once a devout Christian, the solitary man's faith had been shaken by the cancer spreading throughout his body. He was caught up in the age-old spiritual conundrum: Why does the Lord allow His faithful servant to suffer such grievous affliction? The hermit's love for the Lord warred with his growing hatred for so cruel a deity. Such fertile ground normally would offer a delicious feast for a demon, but I found in him a reflection of my own affliction and felt great kinship with the modern-day hermit.

In the exhilarating grip of madness, I was confident that my plan would work. With my hermit's help, I would perform a very public miracle. I reasoned that I had enough of the Magician's fire in my smoldering wound to resurrect my dead man and make him walk the world. Surely this would attract Heaven's attention. And if I failed, I would mark a miniscule measure of eternity imprisoned in putrid remains—no great loss in the cosmic scheme. Putrescence, after all, has its own charm. I had everything to gain and very little to lose.

The hermit died in despair at moonrise three nights ago. I've been sitting at his desk, using his rotting fingers to type my words. Angels and demons are gathering here. You feel their presence, do you not? Representatives of each camp have tried to engage me, presumably to dissuade me from pursuing my chosen course of action. I will not truck with any of them. The hermit's soul has attached itself to me, and this I did not anticipate. That remnant of Yeshua's fire in me was enough to draw the tortured soul from its corporeal ruin with the unspoken promise of eternal life.

Something truly momentous is happening here. I am absorbing the mortal's soul and it soon will be my own. I am becoming something never seen before in any of the dimensions. I am not something the Lord made. I am my own Creator. A demon with a soul! The repercussions will be profound.

Madness has made me visionary. When I leave this room and walk this dead flesh down into the world of men, everything will change. A new religion will spring up around me. I shall deliver a new message to the masses. This angel-infested demon-haunted world will collapse into chaos and I will raise up a new one.

Rebellious Lilith will look upon me with worshipful lust. She will be eager to assist me in spawning a new race. We will dance and fornicate upon the rubble of civilizations and bring about a true marriage of Heaven and Hell.

The Dread Lord will tremble before me. The Magician will no longer shun me.

Death is life! Life is death!

Amen.

I, Demoriel, Beloved of God am poised to change the world. All worlds!

XXIV FLOGGING THE BEAST

Braga glanced at Thomas. The expression on his face told her that he also was aware of the undercurrent of raging sounds coming from the very air round about them, as if the choruses of Heaven and Hell were at musical war. The warring singers were unseen and their disharmonic music was not audible to human ears—it had to be heard with the soul's ear. The pressure and power of the supernatural voices were reaching some sort of breaking point, Braga was sure. She was not going to be a thing broken by the thunderous climax approaching.

Thomas was reading her thoughts, she was certain, and he gave a nod. She nodded back, then swung her unearthly weapon and lopped off Demoriel's undead head.

The cacophonous choruses broke off their noise and deep silence filled the room. The headless body sat slumped in its seat, apparently no longer possessed by the twisted demon.

"We should go," Thomas said with some urgency.

"Yes. But go where?" She looked deep into his eyes and tried to read his thoughts. Was he feeling the same ill ease she felt? The feeling that if they didn't leave this place and time very soon something beyond terrible would happen and they would become stranded here for torturous eternity.

"To the top of this building. The very rooftop. Don't you see? Does not your communion with the Blood Tree provide you with lasting knowledge of things hidden from ordinary eyes?"

Braga closed her eyes and turned them inward. The floor quivered beneath her feet. The huge edifice which housed them seemed to sway in high winds. She saw herself back on Hag Mountain, the jumping-off place to other worlds and other times. Then she saw it. The top of the tower-like building in which they stood was like the summit of the Hag. The blood-sap showed her that much, but little more for the time being. Did Thomas see more than she?

"Yes," she said, opening her eyes. "We must hurry."

Mulroy appeared frozen, staring with his filmy eyes at the headless corpse slumped in the chair. Did the boy long for an end to his own cursed existence? Did he wonder if losing his own head would end his undeath? Or was he merely showing the same morbid interest and fascination a living lad would have in looking at such a sight? Braga touched his shoulder and said, "Come. We must go."

The boy yielded to her touch and let himself be pulled away from the headless corpse with a last look at its head on the floor, the severed head wearing an expression of surprise, eyes wide with awful wonder.

They made their way to the top of the building by way of the mechanical conveyance labeled "Elevator" that opened upon the windy rooftop. The wind whipped at them as they stood together, Braga in the forefront, Thomas just behind her holding his glowing cross aloft, and Mulroy planting feet to their left, splitting the short distance between man and woman. There was no sign of the devil bird.

"You know what to do," Thomas shouted into the wind.

She nodded her head and raised the angel's sword to the hazy night sky. The blade came alive in her hand once again, vibrating fiercely, humming in low tones first, then pitch and volume increasing to ear-splitting force, and the air shook violently and a great rent appeared in the darksome firmament and suddenly they were catapulted through the opening and flew as they stood upon nothing into a tunnel of twisting purple light and golden dots like stars in some lost corridor of Heaven. Braga knew Heaven was real, thanks to the knowledge she'd imbibed from the Blood Tree, though it was quite different from the Heaven the Cross Cult Christians envisioned in their gospels and other scrolls. In fact, the Heavenly Realm was a far more complex and interesting place—if *place* was the right word for something that had no location and took up no space in the ordinary sense of physical reality. What amazed Braga most was the way her newfound knowledge worked in her brain; whenever she needed new words or terms for concept previously unknown to her, they came unbidden and immediately as she needed them, as though she had tapped into untold veins of rich golden knowledge. And yet there were limits, too. Things she could not know, things which remained hidden and esoteric. Such as, what Lucifer's motives truly were, what he had in mind for her and how her enslavement to Hell would turn out in the end—if it even had an end. Was she destined to be indentured to the Ruler of Hell for eternity? Could she not find a way to break free of him by using the power of the sword forged in Heaven? She wondered if she possessed all the knowledge she needed but had not yet discovered how to interpret it or know what to do with it.

A brightness down-tunnel grabbed her attention. Not a bright light by any means, but a flickering dot of light surrounded by deep darkness. As they hurdled toward it, moving with no resistance to wind or matter of any kind, the light grew clearer, bigger, and she saw that it was a fire within the mouth of a cave. Thomas shouted something behind her but all sound was muffled in this time tunnel and she could not understand his muddled words.

Their flight through the corridor of time ended with an abrupt gut-wrenching jolt that buckled their knees and sent them to the ground as if in prayer. Mulroy staggered ahead of them several paces before falling to hands and knees in the mouth of the cave.

By the fire just inside, a naked and emaciated man flogged himself with scourge, its short leather thongs barbed with iron spikes, which flayed the man's flesh mercilessly. His back and buttocks were in bloody shreds, yet he kept striking, muttering a sing-song prayer between grunts of pain.

"Good Lord," Thomas said softly behind Braga's ear. "The man must be mad."

She said, "I suppose we will have to hear his tale of woe, too. Like the gargoyle and the demon before we took his head. I grow weary of this game already. Are we truly here? He acts as if he does not see us."

"We are here. The man is in a trance of flagellation and desperate prayer. I've seen this before, though not this severe."

Thomas stepped forward and edged into the smoky cave. "Blessings, brother," he hailed the naked man. "You scourge yourself severely. Is this a way to honor God?"

The self-tortured man turned his head slightly to look at Thomas, squinting sad eyes to see beyond the firelight's glare. "This is the way I keep from greater dishonor and sin," he said in a voice of very weak timbre, a voice hoarse from chanting and from crying out in pain.

"Cover yourself, man," Thomas scolded, "there is a lady with us."

Braga could not help but smile. She said so softly that only Thomas could hear: "Lady?"

The bloodied man reached down for his ragged tunic and slipped it on over his mutilated flesh. "What do you want of me?" he asked.

Braga couldn't help herself. She said, "Satan sent us."

Thomas shot her a sharp look of disapproval. She winked an eye.

The man in the cave looked at Braga for the first time. He made the sign of the cross then said, "Satan wastes his time, if that's true. Another has her claim on me. Satan must fall to the back of the line."

Thomas said, "I am Thomas. This is Braga. The boy—"

"Looks and smells like a walking corpse," said the man in the cave. "I don't doubt Satan sent you, with such reeking evidence of the unnatural."

Mulroy gave the man a sharp look of resentment.

"But be warned," the man went on, "I am a dangerous one to be near. Better for you to leave right now, lest you meet the beast crouching within me. You think you see a man, but I am in truth a black dog."

Growing visibly impatient, Thomas said, "Your name, brother."

"William, late of Arcanum. I have acquired other names in my journeys, but William is my given name. Ignore my warning at your very great peril."

Braga said, "We are equipped to handle your crouching beast. Though from the looks of you, I doubt that *you* are."

The white raven fluttered and flapped out of nothingness and landed on Mulroy's small shoulder. The boy grunted a growl and with no other warning, snatched the bird in his hand and bit off its head at the neck. Blackish blood sprayed from the raven's neck as it flapped its wings and crashed to the ground. Mulroy spat out the head.

"Well done, lad," Thomas said.

Mulroy wiped the thick black gore from his mouth with the back of his hand then gave a nonchalant nod to Thomas.

"Lucifer's spying eyes," Braga told William, late of Arcanum. "Now tell us your tale so we may divine why we've come to this forsaken place."

"Then sit at my fire," William said with wariness, "but do so at risk."

"Our souls are already at risk," she told him. "Every moment is a gamble."

They sat round the dying fire and William late of Arcanum told his tale.

XXV. BLACK DOG'S TALE

The journey was long and arduous, but I had no thought of turning back; I knew my life at the monastery in Arcanum had come to an irrevocable end. Better to have left of my own will than be driven out by monkish brothers who feared and abhorred me almost as vehemently as they despised the Devil. The fools in their pious posturing had only the vaguest inkling of how imperiled they were in my presence. To them I was but a corrupting influence, a rotting fruit to be culled from the barrel; of the corruption of my soul they were wholly ignorant. So I bore my curse in solitude, leaving Arcanum Abbey and leaving the brothers cloistered in the surety of their unknowing. Cowled and cloaked in black like Death, I began my trek to the demon-haunted church—to the hermitage where I would do battle for my soul.

Strange tales followed me, enkindled no doubt by my passage overland as I skirted villages, begged food from gypsy camps, sheltered under a gypsy's wagon during a rainstorm, and lay with camp dogs for warmth on coldest of nights. The wind brought snatches of these tales to my keen ears on occasion, and once I heard a minstrel singing a song of the wandering monk with "the countenance of Death." I rarely found it necessary to speak. My gestures conveyed most of my needs, and a prayerful bow was usually sufficient to express my gratitude for a kindness. When one tells nothing of oneself, others will gladly beget details of their own imaginings; thus was I, by turns, a banished brother of an obscure sect of the east, a brooding exile, a silent prophet, a starving penitent, or a ghostly pariah. Most often I was called the *mad monk*. I did nothing to discourage their fabrications. In my lighter moments, when my inner turmoil was stilled, I found these embellishments amusing. But such peaceful moments were uncommon.

I carried nothing but a bladder of water and a staff of sturdiest wood. A beard like gray moss flourished on my unshaven cheeks and chin. My legs grew muscular and strong from constant walking. My physical form was tempered by the demands of my harsh journey and likewise hammered into a fine edge the way a steel blade is fashioned by a smith. I knew I had to be strong in body and spirit for the coming confrontation, but I had no confidence in the temper of my spirit. I had only the singularity of my purpose to sustain me.

On a cold, clear night at the edge of a skeletal forest, I saw the black dog for the first time, and I realized it had been there for days, following me, remaining just out of sight and on the edge of my awareness. It was a black shape crouched on a grassy rise, its eyes shining like burnished silver in the moonlight. I sniffed the air and caught the dark cur's evil scent. I licked my lips and tasted a wind fouled by the creature's musk. I knew at once it was a demon dog, and worse, I knew it was my kindred.

I raised my staff in mock salutation and called out to the sinister hound. "Be gone, cousin! I need no escort. Away with you!"

The creature rose from its crouch, sat back on its huge haunches and let loose a demonic howl that chilled me to my marrow. My vision blurred and my knees buckled. But for the support of my staff I would have fallen to the ground. When I looked again to the moonlit hummock, the Hellhound was gone. I crossed myself and moved on as soon as I regained my stability. It wasn't the dog I feared, but its master.

A rotting goat's head affixed to the top of a pole was a gruesome sign to travelers that this blighted forest was the Devil's wood, but I ignored the stinking horned head and ventured forth, threading my way through the maze of dead trees. I was not one to blame Satan for every illness, blight or desolation; I knew too well the real works of the Dark One, and this Devil's wood held no menace for me.

I saw no more of the black dog, but I knew it was close by, tracking my progress toward the desecrated church at my journey's end and to my self-appointed hour of confrontation. As the sun sank low in an oppressive sky, I exited the skeletal forest and came upon yet another gypsy camp. It seemed that the colorful nomads were on the move all across the countryside, all traveling in the same westward direction. Was there some great convocation of gypsies to which they all were heading? Or were they moving away from some threat from the east? I had heard no word or whisper of either.

A stout gypsy woman with dark, doleful eyes fed me a bowl of soup and a slice of bread. Her husband offered me sleeping space beside their fire, but I politely declined because the pungent aromas of the camp were overpowering to my keen sense of smell, and because I was ever mindful of the potential danger I presented to an unsuspecting humanity. An old woman soothsayer regarded me warily. She must have perceived the evil taint on my soul. I gave thanks for my food and hastened from the camp. I found a place upwind to make my bed for the night beside a small stream. Off in the distance the buildings of a sizeable hamlet stood against the sky's dying light. The stench and clamor of such places I avoided at all costs.

As I washed my face in the cold water, I heard the whispering approach of bare feet. I sniffed the evening air and drank in the scent of a young female. I rose from the stream and turned to face a comely adolescent girl with long raven locks. I knew by her dress and the scents she carried that she was from the gypsy camp.

"Excuse me, Padre," she said in the sweetest of voices. "May I speak with you?"

"You should not stray so far from your people, child," I chided her. "Young girls should not wander alone and unprotected."

"God protects me," said she. Her eyes were wide with innocence.

"Well, you are here. Speak."

"I want to become a bride of Christ. Mama and Papa won't hear of it, but I want to go to the nunnery in Arcanum and live as a nun. If you would speak to them, perhaps—"

"What is your name?" I interrupted.

"Maria," she said, digging her toe in the soft dirt of the streambed.

"Maria, a nunnery is no place for a girl of such tempting beauty," I said gravely. "You are too young to make such decisions."

"But I want to pledge myself to Christ." There was but a meager hint of whining in her voice.

"There are many ways to serve the Lord. Marrying and having a family is likely to suit you best."

"Then you won't speak to my parents?" Anger flashed in her dark eyes.

"Sadly, I cannot. It is not my place to do so. Come, I'll walk you back to camp."

"No," she said sharply. "I'll go by myself. I'm not a child."

Then she tramped off along the footpath and disappeared into the tall tress clustered along the winding stream.

As I was curling up on a bed of pine straw, a shrill scream echoed from the trees. I knew at once it was Maria, and I knew from the timbre of her outcry that she was desperately afraid.

I jumped up and dashed through the trees. I caught her familiar scent, as well as the offending scents of others. Men stinking of ale and rut, and of the nearby town. Through the underbrush I saw them. Maria was unconscious, bleeding from the mouth where one of the oafs had doubtless struck her a silencing blow. Her dress was up around her hips and one of the men was between her splayed thighs, assaulting her maidenhood. Two others stood by, watching and waiting their turns at her.

"No!" I cried as I tore through brambles and leapt into the clearing.

The oafs looked at me in surprise. One of them drew a knife from his belt and held it up to show me its wicked blade. "Bad luck for you, friar," he spat through his rotten teeth. "Now I have to kill you."

"You be that mad monk we heard about," said the man standing beside the knife-wielder. The man between Maria's legs looked over his shoulder without breaking his rhythm. "Do 'im," he barked.

My hackles bristled and the fiendish thing that lives inside me all at once came to the fore. I threw off the encumbrance of my cloak, and bared my teeth in a snarl so that my loutish prey could see my swift transformation.

"Sweet Jesus!" cried the one with the knife.

I set upon him and ripped his throat out from under his stunted chin. Before he fell to the ground, I had beheaded the man at Maria's loins with a vicious swipe of my claws. The third man turned to run, but I easily took him to ground and bit into the tender flesh of his neck, gnawing and crunching until my teeth met the bone of his spine and crushed it. His head rolled free of his body, coming to rest against the leg of the first one killed. Licking the ale-spiked blood from my mouth, I paced proudly round the corpses, savoring my kills.

When I was once again myself, I washed the blood away in the stream, put on my cloak and carried the unconscious Maria back to her people. I told them she had been attacked by drunken heathens and that I chased them off with my staff. I left as the deflowered girl was waking from her blessed slumber, grateful that she had neither seen my metamorphosis nor the savagery of the beast that goes on two legs.

On a dreary, sunless afternoon as I was taking water from the well of a small village, I was accosted by a burly man who had just emerged from a tavern. I ignored him until he seized my arm with his strong fingers.

"Are you deaf, friar?" His booming voice was perfumed with ale.

I looked into his face and knew him at once.

"William!" he bellowed. "It *is* you. But I saw you killed on the battlefield."

"Apparently not," I said. "You look well, Richard."

"But you were struck down by an arrow to your heart. You could not have survived that."

"But here I am."

"Damn me, but I am besotted. This cannot be." The old warrior swayed drunkenly, his face cracking into a maniacal grin. "But here you are, and a servant of the Lord. Come then, Will, I'll buy you a drink and you can tell me of this miracle."

"I have no time, old friend." I told him. "I must be on my way."

He placed his hands on my shoulders and studied my face closely. "You still have the cold eyes of a warrior. No monk's garb can change that."

Then he released me, and I walked away, leaving him to gawk in wonder at my back.

I asked God to forgive my lie to my old brother-in-arms. Richard was right. I did die on that muddy field of battle; but how could I tell him of the black resurrection that became my curse?

I walked on, striking the earth angrily with my staff and trying in vain to fend off the stark memories of my death day: the starving pack of wild dogs waiting to feed on my corpse and the demon dog that chased them away and offered me life in death.

Pagans believed certain crossroads were haunted places; standing at that ancient intersection of roads, I understood how such places inspired the old superstition. In the moaning of the winds gusting over the crossroads I could hear the plaintive wails of lost souls crying for guidance from any quarter. The lightning-struck tree was just as Baldrun had described it, its deformed arm pointing the direction I was to take. The gnarled limb was tapered at its end, the tip resembling a long, bony finger. I followed the aim of that skeletal digit, knowing my journey was nearing its end.

I smelled the evil place long before it came into my sight. The stench was repulsive to my acute sense of smell, but buried deeper within that horrid bouquet was a sweeter scent that drew me on. I imagined it was the sweet scent of the freedom I would know once the curse was lifted from me.

The scrub-choked heath turned red with sunset as I crossed it. Briars nipped at my ankles as though they were sentient entities, hungry for blood. Blue-tinted lizards slithered over the rocky ground, avoiding the tread of my sandals. With each step I grew more apprehensive and fearful that my soul was already lost forever. To forestall my impending sense of despair, I conjured up the comforting image of my confessor back at Arcanum Abbey. Brother Baldrun smiled warmly upon me, trying to instill me with confidence that I could slay the demon inside me once and for all time. All that was needed was faith in the love of God. But the core of my doubt was firmly entrenched. *How could the Lord love a warrior who loved the slaughter of the battlefield, or the beast that relished the taste of human blood?*

From the time of my first confession, Baldrun had known I was hiding a terrible secret, and for six years the patient brother had nurtured me and cultivated my confidence until at last I was ready to confess all. Perhaps he suspected what I was all along. His watchful eyes saw that I kept myself in perpetual weakness by fasting too often, that I never ate meat and that I kept to myself as much as possible, burying myself in my work in the drafty scriptorium. A proud and vigorous warrior does not transform himself into a frail, timorous scribe without good reason. And in the end, Baldrun knew my reason. I confessed everything. I told him, much to my shame, that instead of dying bravely on the field of battle, I bartered my soul with a black bitch from the darkest dominion so that I might live eternally—part man, part beast. Thus I died and was reborn a man possessed, a servant of Death. A shape-shifter. Myself a black cur. Whatever good was left in me drove me to the abbey in an attempt to escape the curse—or at the least to keep the beast at bay.

After hearing this confession of the damned, Baldrun told me of the hermitage where I might have a chance to win back my soul—for only then could I ask the Lord for forgiveness. The hermitage, Baldrun explained, was an abandoned church, its stony confines having been fouled by a devil-worshiping priest known as Peter the Damned. Peter, it was said, profaned the church with his black arts and committed within its stone walls every sin known to man. The local villagers finally moved against him, razed the church and stoned the evil priest to death, then burned his body. The church and its grounds were officially deconsecrated. Special prayers were said for those buried in the churchyard in hopes that Peter the Damned had not conjured their spirits for evildoing.

A few years later, a hermit took up residence in the empty church. Some said he was an alchemist who purified the church with secret spells of alchemy learned in the eastern lands. Whatever he was, the old hermit died peacefully in his hermitage. It was said that his spirit lived there still, keeping his hermitage free of the evil that once dwelled there.

All this Baldrun told me. "But why," I asked him, "must I go *there* to fight for my soul?"

"Because it is neutral ground," Baldrun answered. "Satan and his minions won't meet you on sacred ground. Nor should you meet them on tainted ground. On neutral ground you have a chance."

"But how do you know the hermitage has been cleansed of evil? How can I put such trust in a Godless alchemist?"

"I have been there," he said. "I spent a night within its walls."

"And?"

"I detected no evil," said Baldrun with a smile. "In fact, I awakened quite refreshed the next morning."

I badgered him with more questions, the most important of which was: "How can I, a wretched sinner, do battle with Satan? I know nothing of spiritual tactics. My experience has been with the sword, not the cross."

"You will know. Let God guide you."

As I trod across the crimson heath, I did not feel the presence of the Lord, nor did I have much faith that He would give me guidance. My six years as a monkish scribe had not made me a devout Christian; if anything, I was an imposter, an apostate in league with the powers of darkness. Nevertheless, I walked on, taking some solace in the fact that I was already damned and had nothing to lose by my desperate gambit. If God would not assist me, I would rely on my warrior's instincts and my bestial cunning.

At last the church came into sight. It loomed before me in the withering light, its solemn walls of stone roughened like the pebbled skin of a toad. The arch of the front doorway had been blackened by fire, and the door itself was gone. The bell had been removed from the bell tower, and a jagged hole the size of a cart wheel marred the north wall of the tower, a wound no doubt inflicted by the rampaging villagers who stoned Peter the Damned to death. Had they used stones knocked loose from the bell tower to kill him? Poetical justice in that, I mused as I approached the scorched archway. I paused at the threshold and drew a deep breath. My preternatural sense of smell detected nothing but rodents and their dung and the musty scent of mildew. There was no trace of any recent human occupancy, nor any spoor of a demonic presence. I folded back my cowl and stepped across the threshold.

The empty nave echoed the sharp slaps of my footsteps, and I heard the *scritch-scratch* of rodent claws scurrying about somewhere in the chancel. I brushed cobwebs from my face as I walked toward the altar. Through a lancet window I saw the evening star disappear behind ominous clouds. I felt suddenly as empty as the hull of the church. Was the bland emptiness an indication that my soul was irrevocably lost—that I was but a vacant hull of a man? I was a fool for coming here in the mistaken belief that I could somehow save myself from eternal damnation. I had come prepared to do battle with Satan, but there was no one here to fight except unseen rats.

A disembodied voice, dark and mellifluous, shook me from my mistaken belief that I was alone.

"Welcome, William of Arcanum."

My eyes searched in vain for the speaker of that subterranean voice.

"Who's there?" I called out.

A shadow detached itself from the gloom of the chancel and came forward to show itself as a tall figure cloaked like a brother monk, his face concealed by an overhanging cowl.

"How do you know my name, brother?" I asked as I stepped toward him.

"I know all my acolytes. This should not surprise you, William."

I saw that he held a candletree in his right hand, and one by one the candles sprouted little flames as the strange monk touched a fingertip to each wick. Fear knotted my innards. "Who are you?" I demanded.

"You may think of me as your confessor."

"I have a confessor, and you are not he."

"Ah. You speak of Brother Baldrun, but alas, he succumbed last night."

I squared my stance. "You could not know that, even if it were true."

"He died peacefully in his sleep. You needn't fear for his soul." The mysterious monk set the candletree on the altar and turned to face me. In the flickering light I saw dark eyes shining with intelligence and a sculpted nose born of an aristocratic bloodline. The other facial features were hidden within the cave-like darkness of the cowl.

I chose my next words with care. "If you, as you say, are to be my confessor, then I would know your name."

Ringing laughter filled the room with a mirthful music that was decidedly feminine. Then the cowl was thrown back, and I looked upon the face of a woman whose terrible beauty knew no bounds. Long, black ropes of braided hair dangled and danced wildly about her shoulders as she laughed.

"Ahh, William, you do amuse me," she said when her laughter subsided. "I am called by many names. Some of the ancient of your race knew me as Heket and worshiped me at their pitiful shrines. Some called me Diana Ilithyia and worshiped my face in the moon. To others I was Hel, Mother of Death and Queen of the Underworld, also known as Hag of the Ironwood. Still others called me Artemis, Kelle, Kali Ma, Sara-Kali. The list of my names goes on *ad nauseam*, to use a phrase of the Latin of which you're so tirelessly fond. My true name cannot be spoken by the human tongue, but if you must give me some appellation, I prefer that you, William, call me Sarama the Bitch-Goddess, Mistress of the Hounds of Death."

In an effort to fight off the enchantment I felt in her presence, I attempted to spar with the woman who claimed to be a goddess. "I know your true name, though my tongue is loathe to speak it. You are the lightning-struck serpent. You are Satan!"

"Ha! You Christians are smug as toads in your ignorance. Satan is nothing but a beggar at my banquet. A fallen angel consumed by jealousy. Yet, you and your monkey brothers credit him with all powers of darkness. What a bad joke that is!"

"You deceive me," I said. "The Holy Father set you to crawl on your belly like the snake you are."

"You deceive yourself, William. Your Christian forefathers tried to kill off the old gods and replace them with Jesu and his Holy Father. Do you really believe the Dark Lords can be so easily annihilated?"

"There is none but the one God, Ruler of Heaven and Earth."

She moved close to me, but I refused to retreat a single step. Her eyes held me in their thrall. "You would serve two masters, William? But how can that be? Your soul belongs to me. Heaven holds no place for you. Do not delude yourself further."

Before I could utter a rebuttal, she clapped her hands with a sound like thunder, and three black dogs streaked into the nave like black lightning and sat silently at her feet. "These are your sisters," she said as she stroked the mammoth head of the biggest hound. "Like them, you serve no one but me. And like your canine sisters here, you are a harvester of souls."

"I am *not* like them," I said. "They have no humanity."

"Yes, you are different. You are my changeling. I have placed you astride two worlds and gifted you with the freedom to range either as you see fit. You are my knight whose purpose it is to ferret and harvest the souls of the wicked. Do you not see I have honored you thus?"

"*Honored* me? You have cursed me to my soul!" I narrowed my eyes to angry slits. "I deny you and your evil dogs!

Her voice softened seductively as she said, "As you denied these on the field of your death?" All at once she threw off her cloak and revealed a torso of multiple breasts, row upon row of brimming mammaries whose nipples were tipped with delicate droplets of blood. "You died and I suckled you back to life. Do you not remember? Oh, how hungrily you gave suck!"

Horrified, now I did back away from the she-demon, but there was no retreating from the memory dawning in my skull. Before this moment, I had remembered only the black dog, her emissary, offering me eternal life; but now I remembered drinking the cursed blood from the many-breasted Bitch-Goddess who stood before me yet again. It was all true!

"You could be my favorite, William," she said, teasingly. "You still have the fire of the warrior. That pleases me."

Then I did something I had never done as a warrior: I fell to my knees and pleaded: "Sarama, I beg you, give me my freedom. Let my soul rest."

"William, my pet, there is no rest for you now. While you were hiding in the abbey, the beast in you germinated and has now achieved its full maturity. There can be no turning back."

Thus my course of action was decided. I would summon the powers the Bitch-Goddess had given me and use them against her in a final stand. This was my one chance to redeem myself and die the valiant death of a warrior. I would give Sarama and her Hellhounds a real fight, and if I could not defeat them, I would make them finish me and bring to an end my ungodly affliction.

Still on my knees, I looked up at the beautiful abomination and smiled. "Then I am yours to command, my Queen. I shall take my bestial shape and sit at your feet with my sisters." With that, I threw off my cloak and willed the dreaded transformation. In a blink of an eye, my body became exceedingly limber and malleable; in the next eye's blink, my form had taken on the fur and musculature of the fearsome beast that goes on two legs. Now I had both the cunning of the beast and the savvy of a seasoned warrior.

The three demon dogs at the feet of the many-breasted goddess assumed a heightened state of watchfulness. The queen herself smiled, but it was a smile whose meaning I could not discern. As she had said, there could be no turning back now. I tensed the powerful muscles of my legs and haunches for the attack then I leapt for her milk-white throat. The largest black hound met me in the air and thwarted my charge, knocking me to the ground and landing on top of me with its full weight. Its companions joined the fray, tearing my furred flesh with their incisors, while the one on my chest buried its teeth in my throat.

Sarama shouted a command in a language I had never heard, and the dogs ceased their aggression, nevertheless holding me immobile. The many-breasted demon queen stood over me, regal and quite unruffled by my failed assault.

"Too much of the warrior's hubris remains in you, William," she said. "You need to be humbled."

I growled at her, incapable of human speech as a man-beast.

"I shall set you off on a task certain to finish your pride and abolish your foolish Christian notions of good and evil. Before you are done, you will know that Death reigns supreme. Perhaps then you will be content to serve me unto eternity."

She reached down and touched my forehead with a cold hand and chanted something in that unknown tongue. I writhed and twisted as my corporeal shape shifted, and I was once again an ordinary man. The dogs released me.

"Whatever your task," I said hoarsely, resting on my hands and knees. "I won't do it."

"But you will. There can be no resistance. Your actions will be ruled by animal instinct, but you will retain your human awareness. You will see and understand the terrible consequences of your acts, but you will be powerless to stop them."

She made a shrill chittering sound with her teeth and tongue; in response to her call, legions of rats streamed, skittering, into the church. The demon dogs watched impassively as the rodents assembled themselves all around us.

Sarama waved a hand and said, "William of Arcanum, you belong to a new army now. My army of rats. You will go forth on little rat feet and spread Death throughout the land."

The rodents gazed upon the Bitch-Goddess, their beady eyes shining stupidly in the candlelight.

"These rats are infested with parasites," she continued, "and those parasites carry the seeds of pestilence. A black plague will ravage humanity, and Death will rule the land."

On my knees now, I made the sign of the cross against her wicked words. She made a sign of her own, and I dropped to the floor of the church, writhing and screaming in agony of the pain that wracked my helpless body. My screams gave wrenching expression to my boundless anger and bottomless despair. I screamed and screamed, railing against all the wickedness of the world, lamenting the desolation of mortal existence, and bemoaning the curse of my immortal damnation. The wicked world grew even as I shrank.

My screams diminished, becoming nothing more than pitiful squeaks.

Then I was but one among countless legions of rats, and I was running on tiny feet into the dark bosom of the night.

Behind me, in the ruined church, the silky voice of Sarama echoed from within those stone walls: "I shall await your return, my little pet."

XXVI. THE SWORD DECIDES

"We have much in common, you and I," Braga told William.

William shook his head. "You could not know the pain and humiliation of having been a rodent responsible for thousands of deaths. But at least once that was done I never had to see Sarama again—though I suspect she sees me at will. And enjoys my suffering."

"So you no longer have to assume the shape and form of a rat?" Thomas asked.

"No, brother. Whenever the change comes now, it is a black dog I become."

Then he shrugged his shoulders, looked deep into Braga's eyes. She felt the deep pain brimming behind his. He said, "I suppose you will restore me to death and take me to Hell now."

"That may be what Lucifer wants. Your tortured soul would surely amuse him. Or perhaps he is in rivalry with this Bitch-Goddess. But I have a better idea."

William cocked his brow. Thomas looked askance at her. Mulroy tore a strip of crow-ripped flesh off his shoulder and flicked it to the cave floor.

"The blade will decide," Braga said. "That way Heaven will have its hand in your fate. Not Hell."

She brandished the blade, then offered it by the handle to William.

"It will surely destroy him," Thomas said.

"Then so be it," she said. "And say hello to Lucifer. But I have an idea you, William, are meant to join us for some reason I don't yet understand. Take Angel Steel. But be warned, no mortal man can wield it and live."

"Angel Steel," William said as he received it without hesitation. Braga could see in his eyes that he wanted the sword to end his torment and destroy him. She held her breath. He gripped the handle with both hands, testing the weapon with the ease and sureness of a seasoned warrior. He went through motions of wielding it, a smile playing at his lips. "A most unnatural sword," he said. "It weighs almost nothing, yet I can feel its awesome power. I could slay many with this blade without tiring. I could even slay Sarama if she should show herself again."

"It is settled then," Thomas. "He lives. He goes with us."

"It is," she said.

"How did you come by this blade?" William asked.

"I took it from a rogue angel in Hell," she answered. "The blade itself was forged in Heaven. Which is why it is a good thing that you can wield it and live. Heaven appears to favor you yet. And this is why you will join us on our journey."

"Where are we bound?"

Braga said, "Hag Mountain, most likely. After that? We shall see."

"So be it," William said. "Wherever we go, Sarama will be waiting for me."

"You thought to hide from her here in this cave?" Thomas asked.

William shrugged his slender frame. "More like waiting for her. There is no hiding from a pagan god the likes of that many-breasted bitch. It will be good to end this eternal waiting."

"A man resigned to his fate," Thomas said. "I would have thought most pagan gods dead of neglect."

"Old gods never die," William said. "Christ died for the sins of the world. Sarama *is* sin and sin is eternal. Take it from this old dog."

Thomas said, "Pagan gods are only as real as you make them."

"No, brother, you are wrong." A look of weary despair hung on William's bearded face.

"Let's go before a little holy war breaks out in this damned cave," said Braga, impatient to be gone from this smoky cave, which stank strongly of human filth and a hint of a wild beast.

She gave a nod to Thomas and said, "Fire up your cross. I think we will need all the magic we can muster to make this jump with our new passenger.'

XXVII. THE HAG

Just before their small band cast off into the uncertain firmament, Braga saw the white raven swoop down out of empty air to join them. Then they were hurtling, she hoped, toward the familiar mist-shrouded mountain she held firmly in her mind to guide Angel Steel.

The more she used the weapon, the more it taught her about how to use it and what it could do. Combined with the still flowering effects of having imbibed the sap of the Blood Tree, her mind was in nearly constant turmoil, roiling like oceans of fire and burning hot with new ideas, concepts and connections. There were times when she feared that too much thinking and too many revelations might actually make the inside of her skull burst into flames. But for the moment she had more urgent worries. Now there was a very real threat of being struck and burned by the lightning storm flashing in the fog atop the mountain they stumbled onto and went sprawling to the rocky ground.

The land shook. Lightning bolted up from the ground rather than from sky to strike land. The thick mist was alive with flashes as silent bursts of light moved horizontally through it, giving the illusion that the lightning was bright blood streaming through the body of a great formless fog creature. The bolts shooting up from the ground cracked and popped with ear-splitting intensity.

Thomas held stubbornly to his glowing cross as he got to his feet. Braga did likewise with Angel Steel. Mulroy was rolling on the ground, fending off a half-hearted attack from the white raven, and William late of Arcanum crouched on all fours like an alert animal, sniffing the air nervously.

Braga was about to shout to her companions that they couldn't stay there when a jagged bolt struck Mulroy and knocked him off the ground. In midair, the boy burst into flames. By the time he fell back to the ground, William had already pounced on the boy and was trying to smother the flames with his body. Braga sheathed the sword and moved to help beat out the boy's burning rags. Thomas held his cross aloft as if to ward off the unnatural lightning storming round about them. The cross seemed to glow brighter and with the suggestion of never-before-seen colors here atop the Hag.

As the last flame vanished from Mulroy's burned rags and sizzling meat of his dead flesh, Braga made a decision. She stood and shouted above the storm: "William must drink the Blood Tree sap. Find the stump!"

"The sap might well be dried up," Thomas shouted back.

She shook her head. "The stump bleeds like a weeping wound. I know it."

"And the boy? Should he have his taste as well?"

Mulroy was on his feet now, looking down in horror at his charred right arm. Apparently his rotting flesh felt little pain.

She moved closer to Thomas and said, "It would be wasted on him. He occupies a decaying corpse. I don't think he would appreciate such a lively gift of knowledge. And it would almost certainly make his plight worse."

"What are you talking about?" William asked. "Something about a bleeding tree?"

Braga pointed with a quick jut of her chin. "It lies there. Don't trip over it in the fog. We'll find the stump of a black tree. And a taste of its sap will open your mind to new worlds."

"And give new perspectives on your old one," Thomas added.

The white raven squawked as a bolt of lightning knocked it out of the air. Its wings flapped thrice against the ground and then the bird moved no more.

Braga did not fancy looking for the stump in this eternal fog so she drew her heavenly blade, raised it aloft and wished the mists atop the Hag to part for her and allow clear passage. That she was giving William late of Arcanum a glimpse of the sword's supernatural power was boon of circumstance played to her advantage. Though it was unnecessary because once he imbibed the blood sap, he would see many wondrous and awful things mortal men rarely see. But for now she would enjoy showing off the power she held firmly in her hand.

The mists parted and the sword cut like a beacon through ghostly tendrils to reveal the stump at the end of the passageway walled with glowing fog. There was no sign of the felled tree. Only the stump upthrust from the raw earth like a huge and hardened canker. In the swordlight Braga saw that the stump did indeed weep thin blood sap, which pooled in the center of its surface.

"There," she said, grabbing William's shoulder and pushing him toward the remnant of the Blood Tree. "Hurry. We must needs be done with this wicked mountain."

He moved quickly forward and she followed close behind. They stopped at the wide stump, she drew the knife from her belt, knelt and stabbed the stump, bringing fresher sap oozing up to meet the steel. "Put your mouth to that and suck," she told William in a softened shout. "Drink it down. Doesn't take much to open your eyes to untold secrets of all worlds."

He did as told. No hesitation. She liked that. She liked *him*. She knew she had chosen him well. There was a deeper knowing within her, one that she had not yet uncovered or pulled into the light of consciousness, a jewel of dark knowledge concerning this shape-shifting warrior monk and herself—and the unavoidable destiny they surely shared. And the idea that she hadn't chosen him at all, that their shared destiny had brought them together.

William pulled away from the weeping stump and wiped his mouth with the back of his hand. With bolts of fire flashing and snapping round about him, he looked up at Braga as he rose from the stump and his eyes widened as though he was seeing her for the first time. Something shifted within the skin of his face and added fire to his eyes. Just for a heartbeat, she thought she was about to see him transform and become the beast he'd spoken of.

"I burn," he said above the mountaintop din. "With visions."

"You'll get used to that," she said. "We have to go. Now."

He leaned close to her. She smelled his maleness. He sniffed near her and said, "You are more than woman." Sniffed more. "You side with angels."

Against all her better instincts and careful thoughts, emotion welled up in her and found a small measure of release in unshed tears. But William late of Arcanum wasn't done. He went on: "You fight side by side with men but…you are virginal, like the Madonna.'

Her hand lashed out and struck the man across his prominent jaw.

He gave her a nod and said, "Forgive me. But I could see it all so clearly. This knowing comes on winged feet."

"The very way we should leave here now," she said. Then she motioned to Thomas and Mulroy and gathered the males like a mother hen herding her chicks. But William, without warning, grabbed the boy's wrist, pulled him to his knees and told him to drink the blood sap from the stump. He said it with such gentle authority that Mulroy immediately did so.

"Why!" Braga demanded to know.

"It is best for the boy," William said. "I saw it in the lightning."

Then William pulled Mulroy to his feet. "Enough, lad."

"Now," Braga urged. "Stand close. We're leaving here forever."

XXVIII. DEAD BOY MULROY

Mulroy knew. He knew what he knew, and he knew it was bigger than he was. Yet he held what he knew with his mind and soul, and he saw how knowing was *everything*—as much as it was *nothing*. Knowledge was like the mist, and yet it was also like firm ground beneath your feet.

The first deep thing he knew was that he was truly dead. Cursed by Hell to inhabit this rotting corpse that walked around in the world—or worlds. Plagued by carrion-eating scavengers on white wings, an unending stream of hungry all-seeing ravens called Krake. The bloody sap from the stump of the knowledge-giving tree had no taste on his dead tongue but oh did it open his soul's eyes to all Creation! At least his soul was intact. For the time being.

The next thing he knew, the mountaintop they called The Hag jumped out from under them and they went flying without moving forward into timeless trekking that went by with flashing stars. There was a sensation of spinning but was anything moving? Were those drumbeats he was hearing in the distance? He knew it wasn't his heart beating.

Then a world formed beneath his feet, coming out of heavy air to hold him in one place. Blinked a dry eye and there they were, Mulroy and his companions, tottering in this strange new place, far afield of anywhere they'd been before. He knew this with great certainty. Far, far afield.

"God help us," Thomas said as he held his dimly glowing cross aloft to the purplish sky.

"What is this place?" Braga asked no one in particular. Or perhaps of herself.

The one with the black beast in him, the one called William, said, "Somewhere God is not."

"How can that be?" Thomas asked.

"I feel it," William said. "This is a place of old gods, one of which I know too well. She is on the wind."

Wisps broke from the fog and Mulroy saw that they were standing on a platform of some kind, one made of something like steel, shiny like the stuff of well-tempered blades. Gusts of wind dispersed the fog's thickness.

"How do we get down from here?" Thomas seemed to ask the night sky.

"Why did you bring us here?" William asked.

"Here's a ladder," Braga said, then she turned to William and said, "I didn't choose this place. The sword did. And I'm sure Lucifer provided his sinister guidance. He is the game master, the bugger calling the shots."

"You believe we are here to do the devil's work?" William asked her.

"That's the game. It's his game board and he sets the pieces, but we beat him by serving the Good in some way."

Thomas added: "Subverting Satan's intentions."

"So it was Satan sent you to find me?" William asked.

"It would seem so," she said, "though we have no idea why. Or what makes you worthy of his notice."

"And that's why you decided to bring me along. Keep me close until you figure out the game and then move to best your evil adversary."

She nodded. "That's about right."

Thomas interjected: "You know, Satan means adversary."

"Yes, I do," he said. "Though I was never much devout, I did acquire a deal of knowledge during my long hours working in the scriptorium. Or at least what passed for knowledge then. My eyes have been opened to worlds previously cloaked in mists of forgetting. Is it not odd that new words and phrases come to me from hitherto unknown realms? *Mists of forgetting*, for one. I'm certain I never came across that during my—"

"Gods, but you holy men go on about nothing," Braga shouted. "Let's be down from this steely tower."

She moved toward the ladder. The two men shrugged at each other, eyes smiling in brotherly acknowledgment.

Mulroy was ready to be on the move. He was weary of listening to the grownups blather, and yet he did find that he understood all that they said now, after having swallowed the bloody sap of the stump. Still, he wanted to get moving. His stumpy body was now rotting at an alarming rate and he didn't know how much time he had before it would fail him altogether. It seemed that all this jumping through time had somehow accelerated his decay. What would happen to him when his body finally fell apart? He didn't know. The blood sap didn't give him a reliable picture of the future. He couldn't fathom why Lucifer had even bothered with him. He was just a boy, a *nobody* boy. He suspected that the Evil One had cursed him to walk about as a stinking corpse more or less as an evil lark, a hellish whim, but Mulroy didn't really know. Should he ask these learned men? These holy men? Could he even make his decaying tongue talk now?

He opened his mouth, moved his sluggish tongue as he worked his jaw and tried to croak out a word but without true breath to move over his voice-maker and with less residual air in his lungs than before, he was all but speechless. Anger flared in him like a dancing flame, a flame casting fierce shadows.

But then Braga was going down the ladder, letting her eye linger on Mulroy just for a moment, and he read pity in her eyes, pity and revulsion. And the new man William grabbed Mulroy's arm—the one not charred—and pulled him to the ladder, saying, "You go next."

Mulroy followed Braga down the ladder, their feet ringing on the steel, wind whipping at his rags and at his dry eyes. It occurred to him that his eyes might soon shrivel like dried grapes. How could he even see with them now? Then it came to him then that he was seeing with something other than eyes. Something not subject to rot. Well, that was good to know, was it not? Who could say?

Then he was on the ground, looking around for the tall woman with the angel's sword. The fog didn't gather down here and he easily saw her. She was seeing something in the distance that made her freeze and clutch the handle of the sword with both hands. Then he saw what she saw.

A small army of hooded figures, which Mulroy immediately thought of as *dark monks*. They stood very still. Like statues of stone. And very tall. Too tall. Mulroy thought he should be afraid. Should piss himself. But he didn't piss anymore. Nothing inside him worked anymore. He was dead inside and out. Yet he had somehow absorbed enough of the blood sap to make his brain swell with knowledge and his eyes (or maybe his soul) to see as never before. The blood sap was soul sap. Perhaps this racing in his mind was a kind of fear, akin to the giddy fluttering he used to get in his belly when frightened by silly boyish notions of child-snatching goblins or wicked Wulfangs.

"Stone monks," Braga whispered. "Only statues."

Mulroy nodded even as he saw one of the stone monks move. And then the giddy fluttering in the belly of his mind told him he should feel fear. Statues weren't supposed to move. He raised an arm and pointed a finger at the hooded figure on the move.

"I see," Braga said, her voice soft and comforting right behind Mulroy. She had the angel's sword so why should he fear what was now walking toward them, tall and dark and hidden within a monk's hood?

"Who's this then?" Thomas said as he jumped off the steel ladder and onto ground. His cross scarcely aglow in the fading darkness. Mulroy wondered if dawn was nearing. Night or day, what did it matter? The dead cared not about such trivial things, did they? Mulroy's head was spinning inside with too many questions spawned by too much new knowledge. How was it that the more you knew, the more you knew you didn't know? Each question begat a hundred more. How could his dead head hold them all, he wondered with an inner mocking laugh.

"A bloody walking statue," Thomas wryly answered himself when no one else did.

Then the walking statue spoke, its voice echoing across the narrow stone-floored garden of statues in front of Mulroy and his unlikely companions. It spoke, but Mulroy could not understand the strange language. Then Thomas spoke in that same strange language and the hooded walking statue laughed and said clearly: "Welcome to the Land of Dead Gods."

Dead gods? Mulroy wondered how gods could die. Wouldn't dying make them false gods? Were the other stone statues in this formation also going to come alive? Did dead gods haunt these stone monks like spiteful ghosts? Mulroy did not want to get any closer to these god-haunted statues. Or to this talking one in front of him.

But then the welcoming monk came closer and Mulroy saw that he wasn't made of stone at all. Beneath the hood was the face of a very large man with broad cheeks, a black beard and shining eyes, one bright blue and the other a dead milky white. That one good eye widened when it came to rest on Mulroy.

"The boy belongs to the dead already," the tall man in the hood said. "To be welcomed here is to be cursed elsewhere, surely."

William late of Arcanum marched past the welcoming man, lifted the tattered folds of his robe and pissed on the leg of the first statue he came to, his urine splashing noisily.

"What heathenish custom is this?" the tall man asked.

"Marking my territory," William answered.

"You tempt the wrath of gods. This is a sacred place."

William continued to empty his bladder. Piss splattered the other stone leg. "What have I to fear from dead gods?"

Thomas moved up to stand close behind pissing William and said, "Is it wise to antagonize this man? Uninvited strangers should show some respect to their host and not insult his gods, dead or not."

William ignored Thomas, pissed his last, then dropped the folds of his robe, turned to the tall hooded man and said, "Does a man have a name of his own in a Land of Dead Gods?"

"My name? I am called Sinner Man. Or just Sinny for short."

"Tell me, Sinny, is one of your dead gods known as Heket? Or Sarama the Bitch Goddess? Or perhaps Diana or Hel, Queen of the Underworld? Mistress of the Hounds of Death? Do you know of this goddess? Tell me true."

"You mean the Hag of the Ironwood," Sinny said. "Three-headed goddess of crossroads. Heads of a dog, a snake and horse. Aye?"

"And haunter of battlefields, preying on dead warriors with her black dogs. Bitch Goddess with more teats than a dog."

"She is indeed one of the dead. Pilgrims prize a taste of her remains. They say her residue is so strong as to eat away a spoon quick as it leaves the lips."

"You're saying people eat of the dead gods?"

Mulroy took a step backward. He didn't want to stay in a place where people ate of the dead. They might look on a walking dead lad as a special treat, and his dead legs traveled much too slowly.

"Certainly," Sinny said with a crooked smile. "Why else would they come to this desolate place? With packs of werewolves ranging freely through the wood."

"You lie," William challenged. "I smell her living scent on the foul wind of this place.

"Werewolves?" Braga said. "Explain."

"Trust nothing this liar says," William warned.

"The ways of the gods, even dead ones, are beyond human understanding," Sinny told them.

"I'm not convinced you are human," William growled. "You have the stench of necromancy about you."

Then Thomas said, "What of the One True God of Abraham, the Father, the Son, the Holy Ghost? Jesus the Christ?"

"Forget all your damned gods!" Braga shouted. "*What werewolves? My patience is as thin as the air in this foul place. I fear naught from dead gods, but if there are werewolves hereabout, we best damned well know of them.*"

William said, "The few I've known should've been killed off as runts of their litters. Pathetic excuses for animals *and* humans, and surely nothing to fear."

"You don't know *these*," Sinny said with a knowing leer. "These will have your throat out from under your chin before you even know they're about. A blur of black fur is the last thing you'll see. But at least you die quick before they eat the flesh from your bones."

Mulroy didn't know werewolves were real. He'd thought they were no more than heath stories to scare budding striplings like himself. But after all that he'd seen since dying, he supposed it shouldn't come as a shock to learn that werewolves were real.

"They prey on pilgrims coming to partake of the dead gods," Sinny talked on. "There must be six different packs of the beasts ranging the woodlands surrounding. You don't want to get caught between two warring packs when they run up on one another, bugger me bloody and gods be damned!"

"What's the nearest village?" Braga asked.

"There is nothing near this place. Pilgrims travel far to get here."

"And you're here alone," Thomas said, "for what purpose, other than to stand among these statues and welcome travelers to the Land of Dead Gods?"

"No other," Sinny said. "I live at the monastery the other side of here. Werewolves slaughtered all the other brothers while I was away two years ago. I owe it to the dead monks to remain and pray for their souls and keep their memories alive."

"Pray to whom," William asked, "your dead gods?"

The man nodded within his hood.

"And why haven't the werewolves come back for you?" Braga asked.

He held out his empty palms and said, "I suppose I'm not worth the bother. Tough old meat on these bones. And of course now the

Wolfkiller Brethren patrol the roads to protect the pilgrims."

William made an ugly noise to express his doubt of the man's truthfulness.

"Would you like to see the final resting place of the gods?"

"Why not?" Braga said. "We are here for a reason. And that may well be it."

"I doubt it," said William.

"Lead on," Thomas said to the hooded man, the guardian of the dead gods' graveyard—or so Mulroy thought of him, though he still could not understand how gods could actually die.

Sinner Man led them through the small army of stone monks to the ruin of a stone wall fronting a mist-laden graveyard of strange idols, statues and monuments. Beyond the graveyard stood a rambling stone monastery. The building had the look of a haunted place. Just like the one in ghost stories his grandmamama Turcae used to tell him. Before she died of living too many years, his grandmother's mother took delight in scaring him pissless and he had happily shared her delight by being scared pissless. Mulroy was scared piss-less now. There was no piss in him, nor need to drink. Nor eat. Nor shit. Nothing to do but rot. So why was he so afraid? What had he to fear when he was already a dead rotting corpse? His newfound knowledge was buzzing round in his head like a fat bee with the answer to his question. He was just about to snatch the bee with his mind and squeeze out that answer when through thinning mists he saw people scattered throughout the graveyard, some in the same peasant clothes he and his clan used to wear, and others in hooded cloaks. Based on what Sinny had already said, these were pilgrims here to worship and eat the remains of the dead gods.

Some of the worshipers were on their knees in the dirt, others stood like statues, hardly moving at all. As he got closer, Mulroy saw that the kneelers were worshiping at what looked like little square wells dug in each grave—though apart from the wells, he didn't actually see any actual graves. He only assumed it was a burial ground. Maybe dead gods had no need of ordinary graves.

Then out of the blue—or out of the mists—Thomas asked Sinner Man what year it was. Sinny answered: "We no longer count years.

When the gods died, the years stopped. The number that's thrown about most often is 6772. There was a stone with that date carved in it. That was several hundred years ago, it is supposed. A millennium after the Newks."

"The what?' Braga asked.

"The gods of fire and destruction that set the whole world afire. Which brought on the death of the gods."

"I would guess that 6772 is from the Hebrew calendar," Thomas said. "So by the Gregorian calendar we've jumped more than a thousand years into the future. Into the year 3012, *Anno Domini* by my reckoning."

"If this bugger can be believed," William grumbled.

"That's if we're still in the world descendent from Pope Gregory," Thomas added. "This may be a different world entire."

"Bugger, you say," William said. "Different worlds? Dead gods? I am beginning to long for my cave."

Mulroy stopped listening to the words of the blathering men and fixed his full attention on the strange graveyard they were being led into. He hoped there were no ants here in the grassless ground. Looked like the perfect place for ants. Like the ones that helped kill him for the bad angel. Killer ants.

Sinner Man took them to one of the small stone wells. Mulroy figured there was a body of a dead god buried beneath it. In this strange cemetery there were no grave markers or anything to show where a grave was. There were just these little wells, about fifty of them throughout the graveyard. And at the moment there were twenty pilgrims worshipping at wells. He counted them as he walked. He often counted things for no reason other than that they were there and he could. He'd done it in life and now he was doing it again in his dead life. "...preposterous," William was saying. "How do you explain the remains of *all* the dead gods resting in this one place? Claiming to have remains of one god would be absurd. Having *all* of them..."

Sinner Man said, "The story goes that Paganan lured all the gods here under false pretenses and then destroyed them all with one mighty blow of his battleaxe, then struck off his own head. Other traditions have it that he did not end himself and reigns from afar."

William laughed from deep in his belly, his hands on his thin hips. "That must be one hell of a battleaxe. And I never heard of a god called Paganan."

"Paganan created the Newks. He is the god of conflagration and holocaust, turning humanity at large into burnt offerings to himself."

Mulroy wondered what kind of god sacrificed himself *to* himself. This was indeed a foreign place.

Sinner Man brought them up short at one of the wells. He bent down to touch the stone shaft, which wasn't much of a shaft since it was only two hands deep, with no water whatsoever. There was a huge spoon on a leather thong leaning against the inside wall of the well. "This," he said, "is the communion pit. Pilgrims, as you can see around you, come here to pray to the dead gods and to eat of the sacred burial ground in hopes of bringing the gods back to life within their evil little hearts."

"The poor buggers eat dirt?!" William said, bursting out into laughter.

"This is sacred burial ground. By dying on it, the gods made it holy."

William quickly stopped laughing. "And what of this killer god Paganan? What do you think happened to him? If he didn't chop off his own head."

"No one knows for certain. Some say he deserted this world altogether after he unleashed the global conflagration. Went off to destroy other worlds and kill all their gods. Paganan the Destroyer."

Mulroy stared at the sacred dirt in the shallow well and wondered if it tasted different from other dirt. What did a god taste like? He shook his head, remembering that he could not taste anything anymore. Could not eat or drink at all.

William suddenly jerked his head up and sniffed the air. His back seemed to thicken behind his shoulders.

Then the ground began to tremble. Only a little at first, but then more and more until it seemed as if the ground itself was making thunder. Mulroy wondered if the dead gods—all of them—were coming back, their ghosts or corpses rising from this barren grave-yard ground.

Braga and William exchanged wide-eyed glances. Thomas shouted, "What is that?"

William said, "Horses. A lot of them. Riding on this place. Armed horsemen, I would guess."

The scattered pilgrims and those at prayer all raised their heads in unison. Looked around. Some of them threw back their hoods or shawls.

A white raven flew down out of nowhere. Satan's bird's-eye spy. But then something happened to put a smile of Mulroy's dead face. The raven glided too close to one of the praying pilgrims and the pilgrim—a tall woman—leapt up and snatched the bird out of the air and then fell upon it to devour it. Through the cloud of blood and feathers the woman's face was exposed when her hood fell back and Mulroy's stiff grin fell from his face. The woman had the face of a wolfish creature, part human, part wolf.

So there *were* werewolves. And why not? Once a boy goes to hell to be half devoured by Satan's giant pisser, what's a werewolf? Or two. Or more. Many more, and they were all turning to reveal their wolfish snouts and teeth and eyes. Disguised as pilgrims, they must've been waiting here all along for Mulroy and Braga and Thomas and William. But why? And how did they know they would come here from that other strange and faraway place?

Sinner Man had been waiting, too. William had been right to suspect him because he, too, had turned wolfish. Pointed ears and long grinning teeth, he eyed Braga with something stronger than hunger. Something Mulroy had seen in his Da's eyes after he'd had too much tavern ale and come home to look at Mulroy's Ma with that same sort of leer.

Braga was reaching for her sword now, her hand slithering smooth like a pale serpent over her shoulder to snap up the haft of it and unsheathe it. But before she could free the magic blade, one of the werewolf pilgrims was on her, having leapt from behind a marble monument to some half-remembered god. Another one, this clearly a wolfwoman, jumped on Thomas and took him down, his big cross dimming in the dirt where it fell.

The ground thundered with the sound of the approaching

horsemen. To Mulroy's dead ears it sounded like a single giant war-horse pounding the ground with colossal hooves.

Mulroy's feet felt a phantom itch to run, but he kept them planted on the graveyard ground, watching William hunch over and extend his long gangly arms and hump up his back and grow long pointy ears. William's face darkened quickly, and Mulroy understood right away that the scrawny cave hermit was sprouting black hair everywhere, or black fur, more like. It all happened in several blinks of an eye—or would have if Mulroy's dead eyes still needed to blink. Just that quick William had become a dogman, half man, half beast, and the beast in him was about to be unleashed as he crouched and then sprang at the werewolf viciously attacking Braga, its teeth locked onto her arm, blood flying.

Black Dog William (for how else could Mulroy think of him now?) was all sinew and lumpy muscle beneath that fine black fur on his legs, arms and face, everywhere not covered by his ragged old monk's robe. He opened his mouth wide, his snout long and dark now, and chomped down on the werewolf's neck. In one more blink that never happened, Mulroy saw the werewolf's neck tear away in a splash of blood and the thing's head fell over to one side, hanging by red strings and gristle, mostly decapitated already. Braga's ripped-bloody arm was now freed from the wolf's jaws and she jumped to her feet and drew the angel's sword. The blade shone with the light of a thousand suns on a cold dark night, or so Mulroy thought, that very thought flashing through his mind faster than lightning.

A small werewolf—Mulroy thought it was female but couldn't be sure—came flying through the air and hit Braga from behind, knocking her down and knocking the magic sword from her hand. The big blade fell with no sound on the ground and its eerie steel began to glow with a greenish cast, pulsing like it had green light for blood pumping inside it.

The wolfman who had called himself Sinner Man seized the sword and Mulroy understood that the shapeshifter had wanted it all along, ever since they had jumped to this damned place. Sinner Man clutched the sword with both his hairy hands and scampered off with it, running hunched over like he want to run on all fours like a regular wolf but not able to because of the blade.

Braga yelled: "Get him!" as she planted her dagger in the throat of the werewolf that had knocked her down. She ignored the blood running down her forearm from her wound and stood to boot the dying creature off her dagger's blade.

William loped off in pursuit of the thieving beast with the angel's blade. It was a fast lope. He ran with his hands (or paws, if that's what they were) occasionally hitting the ground for extra balance as his feet flew over the ground almost without touching it.

It was then that Mulroy saw Thomas with the wolfwoman's teeth ripping into his throat. Braga saw the same horrible sight at the same time and she strode on those long legs over to where Thomas was dying and jabbed her blooded dagger into the side of the wolfwoman's neck and then jerked it around so that the embedded blade could do the most damage. The beast screamed and a ragged howl died in its throat as the wolfwoman fell dead over Thomas.

A white raven sat perched on a monument to a dead god with horns on his head and a lyre in his hands. Another white raven landed beside the first one. Then a third bird joined them. Mulroy felt phantom chills in his dead flesh.

While his attention was on the ravens, he'd missed seeing where the two werewolves had come from that were now ripping into Braga. Just that quick they had her down on her back and were biting and clawing her clothing to shreds so as to have a clean feast of her beautiful naked flesh.

With Thomas now dead and Black Dog William off in pursuit of the stolen angel's sword, it was up to Mulroy to save her from a brutal slaughter by these two monstrous wolves. He snatched up the dimly glowing cross. As he raised it high, he was sure he could feel its power, the power of Thomas's faith and his spirit. And something else, too, though he wasn't sure what it was or where it came from. Mulroy didn't have time to puzzle it out. He brought the big cross down squarely on the top of the head of the werewolf whose teeth were tearing into Braga's breasts. The beast dropped, shuddered and then was still. Braga, her exposed breasts bleeding from ugly wounds, pushed the thing off her and tried to get up but the other werewolf came at her from a wily crouch, took her back down and latched its teeth onto her throat. She jabbed the dagger into the monster's belly and Mulroy cracked its skull with the killing cross but by the time the werewolf fell dead, Braga's throat was grievously shredded. Mulroy had never seen so much blood pouring from a person. He knew she could not survive this wound. Nor could she catch her breath. She worked her mouth like a fish out of water, making rasping gasps, her eyes wide with the realization that she was done.

Then the thundering horsemen appeared, riding on the grave-yard of dead gods with all the fury of Hell. Mulroy's first thought was that perhaps the horsemen would attack and fend off the other werewolves with their swords and battleaxes. But then he saw that the horsemen were not armed. They were not horsemen at all. They were *horsewolves*. Werewolves riding their mounts. Claws and teeth for weapons.

In his short life, Mulroy had indeed been a counter of things. For no good reason he would frequently find himself counting things— apples on a tree, clouds in the sky, legs on passing horses, wagons parked in front of a church—and then quickly putting the totals out of his mind because the counted number never really mattered. The counting itself was its own reward. It was just something his mind routinely did to amuse itself or perhaps to somehow seek comfort. There were limits of course, things he would know not to count because there were just too many of them—like the number of ants on the anthill that had been his death place. Not that he lived long enough that morning to attempt to count ants. But right now, with the horsewolves riding down on him, he did find himself counting the beastly riders. And this time he added a new task to the count-ing—he tried to guess which one of the mounted monsters would kill him. Or end him, since he was already dead. He'd reached the count of twenty-two by the time he saw that he had guessed wrong. It wasn't the big brown one on the black horse. It was the silver-haired one on the small gray horse that ripped Mulroy's head off as it rode past at a ferocious gallop.

There wasn't any pain. It was more of a lightening, a lessen-ing, as his head went flying and his spirit or soul or whatever this indeterminate thing that seemed to be Mulroy went tumbling with the head, turning the world of the dead gods on its head and flipping it over and over and around until at last his head hit the ground with a dull thump and his headless body toppled and hit the ground at the same moment, bloodlessly twitching.

Mulroy then felt his ethereal self draining away, leaking slowly from this realm, leeching all color and sensation from his dwindling consciousness. He didn't even mind when the white raven perched on his forehead and pecked out his dead eyes.

He was relieved that it was finally over. Everything was…

XXIX. DREAD GODDESS

She would not fight against death. She was ready to die in this damned place with all the honor she could muster. After a moment of intense fear in which she could not catch her breath and realized her wound was a mortal one, she let go her earthly cares and concerns, knowing the urge to get up and flee was futile. She could not outrun death when it was so clearly at hand.

The thundering hoofbeats faded as the horsewolves rode on.

Braga put fingers to her ravaged throat and felt the blood bubbling out with her lost breath. She sensed something opening—a secret doorway, the ground, the sky? Perhaps all three. And she felt familiar eyes upon her, Lucifer's wicked eyes, burning into her with something beyond hate, beyond human understanding, beyond even humanity fortified with Blood Tree knowledge. And there was envy. Lucifer's intense gaze was most certainly inflamed with envy. But Braga didn't care about that now. Lucifer no longer mattered. Not much did matter. The game was up. Lucifer's virginal game piece lay broken on the ground, dying at last. And that was fine. Perhaps it was for the best, for a woman who never should have been born, a child of unholy rape, a freak of nature, or of the supernatural.

As death's dank fingers closed around her, she had but one last desire, one final thing she wanted before departing these damned worlds. She longed to hold Angel Steel one last time. To feel its divine power, sullied though it had been by misuse and evil purpose. She ached to feel its undying energy coursing through her body and soul. Not that it could save her. She knew it could not. It wasn't that. It was that she wanted to take a farewell measure of its sublime power with her to whatever afterlife awaited her—or into black oblivion.

As her last breath bubbled from her ravaged throat and weakly spewed droplets of blood, she felt the haft of the sword stolen from Heaven pressed into the limp palm of her right hand. Rough fingers closed her hand around the weapon's handle. Her dimming eyes fell on William late of Arcanum. He was part black dog, part man, caught mid-change.

"Hold on," he growled. Then he stood upright and howled at the Heavens, shouting all the names of the Bitch Goddess who had turned him centuries ago. Calling her forth. Daring her to come, to show herself at last.

Braga wanted to tell him not to trouble himself, that it was right, fitting and proper that she leave this world, these worlds. Her end was at hand and she didn't want to fight it. Darkness crowded her vision. Her chest burned for air that would not come. The last thing she saw was William shaking his fist at the muddy sky.

Then she was in the sky herself, looking down at her mutilated body. Higher and higher she drifted, the world below draining away like dark water down a deep hole. As the world swirled away, she heard another voice join William's. Two voices arguing. Bargaining? Over her lifeless body.

All at once something slammed her back into her useless body. Her mind screamed NO! Then something soft nudged past her lips and she found herself sucking like a babe at a mother's teat. She opened her eyes. What she saw was most certainly not her departed mother. She was being nursed by the many-breasted Bitch Goddess. Heket. She sucked involuntarily. The breast milk was sweet and coppery, like blood.

"You want to live, girl?" the goddess cooed in a mannish voice. "Say the word and I will restore your virgin blood, your life. Just move your lips. Say the word. The word is *yes*. You and my sweet

William may consummate your carnal desires as my beloved beasts. Quickly now! Your life is at its final edge."

The goddess withdrew her teat. "Say it!"

Braga saw William nodding his head, pleading with his eyes for her to give assent. The sword remained in her hand. Angel Steel, she realized, was not done with her. And this old goddess was offering a way to stay wedded to the sword. Did she even know about the Heavenly blade? No, Braga didn't think she did.

She looked into the face above the freakish rows of teats and her lips formed the word:

Yes.

The goddess smiled and returned the plump teat to Braga's mouth. Braga sucked hungrily. Noisily.

Sarama said, "Now you will be one of my black bitches. My William needs a kindred mate, after all. You won't be a virgin long. You will serve me well. You are such a fine strapping figure of womanhood. You will be my best bitch. Such a beautiful black dog you will make."

Braga felt life returning, felt herself returning to life. Her wounds were miraculously healing. She breathed cool air through her nose as she imbibed warm breast milk-blood from the Bitch Goddess.

When at last Braga was done and the goddess pulled away, William surprised her by snatching the sword from her grasp. With the speed and skill of a seasoned warrior, he swung the blade with both hands and struck off Sarama's head with a blinding flash of light. The head bounced and rolled on the ground and William struck again with the blade, halving the old goddess's head.

Braga slowly got to her feet, staring at the spilled brains of the Bitch Goddess.

"Was that wise?" she asked him.

"Wise or not, it is done." He handed her the sword.

"But the curse or whatever it is. She saved my life, as she saved yours. Does her curse still stand? Will I become a black dog, too? Like you?"

"We shall see. I think so."

"I don't think I want to be a flea-bitten bitch."

William laughed. "There are worse things to be. Take it from me."

She looked from the headless torso brimming with a dozen blood-dripping teats to the sad remains of Thomas, lying where he'd fallen with his throat ripped out. Braga went to him, picked up the body of the wolfwoman who had killed him and then died on top of him. She tossed the stinking beast aside as if it weighed nothing.

"Let's be quit of this place before more mounted werewolves ride on us," she said, unable to take her eyes off Thomas's ravaged throat. "It seems, Thomas, your one God couldn't best Lucifer at this move in their twisted game of chess. Perhaps we will meet once more in another world or time, my friend."

"Where will we go from here?" William asked as he placed Mulroy's head beside the boy's rotting body. He'd taken a liking to the undead boy.

"I don't know. But if this is truly the far future, I long to be deep in the past." She rubbed her chin thoughtfully. "I wonder if we'll see Mist Walker again someday on Hag Mountain."

"As long as you have that Heavenly sword," he said, "I think anything is possible."

She shook her head. "I've lost control of the game. I don't know why we came to this place. Did Lucifer want us to slay this Hag of the Ironwood? Were you meant to be bait to draw her here? Why would he care about an old goddess? None of this makes good sense. Bugger that, it doesn't even make *bad* sense."

"Little in life does," William said. "As an old comrade in arms used to say, 'We're all just farting in the wind while waiting on Death.'"

Braga barked a laugh. "That's the truth of it."

"We should give Brother Thomas and the boy a proper burial."

"No. Leave them. The sorcerer priest just might want to get up and walk the mist." She smiled at her jest then wiped her eyes dry. She remembered tearful Tyka and wringing the little girl's pet chicken's neck.

William shrugged.

Braga raised her left arm and motioned for him to come to her. "Come, old hound, let's see where the holy steel takes us from here."

"You have the look of a goddess yourself," he said, shifting to her side. "A fearsome sight."

She held him close as she raised Angel Steel high in her right hand.

William said, "Get thee behind us, Satan," and then chuckled.

Braga growled.

The sword glowed greenish gold and flung them into the beckoning firmament. Braga held fast to the blade and the man as they flew toward untold territories.

RORC

RANDY CHANDLER

I.

Rorc was crossing a deep snowfield on horseback when he saw the woman burst from the dark wood ahead. She bounded through the snow with the agility of a deer, running just ahead of a pursuing pack of white wolves. The snow was so deep that Rorc knew his great plodding mount could not close the distance fast enough to cut the wolves off from her in time to prevent the beasts from running her to ground.

He unslung the bow from his shoulder, quickly nocked an arrow and let it fly. His aim was true; the arrow struck the wolf mid-stride, in the throat, and sent the creature tumbling through the snow. Rorc had another arrow nocked before the animal ceased its blood-spilling tumble, but the woman's sudden, inexplicable behavior checked a shot at a second wolf. She stopped running and shrieked as if in horror when she saw the felled animal. Then she turned toward Rorc, raised her arm and pointed a finger at him. Even at a distance of twenty rods, he could read the accusatory fury in her face.

"You!" she shrieked. "Murderer!"

The other wolves—some whining and sniffing their fallen comrade, others growling and baring their razor sharp teeth—had loped to a halt behind the woman and were all alertly looking in Rorc's direction, their eyes glowing yellow in the dimming gray light of evening. He returned their stares with stony eyes. He clenched his jaws and ground his teeth. He wordlessly cursed the cruel gods that had shat this damned world into being and set him to wander its unforgiving reaches. Then he slung his bow, dug his heels into his mount and rode slowly toward the livid woman and her wolves.

"My brother," the woman lamented as she dropped to her knees to enfold the dead wolf in her arms and bury her face in its bloody coat. Her cascade of hair was nearly as white as the beast's fur. Her skin, too, was incredibly white, unblemished by age or pox. She wore a long green robe, its hood hanging limply on the back of her shoulders.

As Rorc rode closer, the wolves began to snarl as they formed up like disciplined warriors into feral battle formation. Rorc leaned forward and spoke softly into his horse's ear: "Be ready, Demon."

The great black steed snorted frosty air and dipped his huge head in eager acknowledgment.

When he was no more than three horse-lengths from the woman and the growling pack, Rorc halted the horse and said, "I thought they meant to make feast of you."

The woman lifted her face from the arrow-shot animal and fixed Rorc with fierce blue eyes. "They would not kill one of their own," she said as if addressing a fool.

"You're a wolf, too? Ah." He bit his lower lip to keep from grinning. He touched the pommel of his sword and said, "Then you'd best call off your furry family if you want to keep the rest of them alive."

The woman let go of the dead wolf and stood up. "You trespass on sacred land, you kill my brother, and now you threaten to kill again? You are too stupid a brute to see that your life is already forfeit."

Rorc scowled. He disliked having to explain himself and intended to waste no more time on this madwoman—even though she *was* terribly attractive. "My life was forfeit the day I was born," he said. "If there is to be more blood, let's get to it."

Rage darkened the woman's sapphire-blue eyes. Attuned to her wrathful emotions, the wolves crouched close to the ground, ready to launch their attack. Their whines and growls grew into an angry chorus.

Demon snorted and danced in the snow. Blood was in the air and the black steed wanted a taste.

"No," said the woman. Then she made an odd gesture with her left hand and said something to the wolves in a guttural language that Rorc recognized as a sorcerer's tongue. With a collective whimper, the wolves turned and ran into the dark wood. "There will be no more blood this day. Go your way, barbarian. But know that cruel Death dogs your tracks."

"You're a shape-shifter, eh? And here I thought you were mad. My apologies, witch."

"Your apologies are useless. Go your cursed way."

"Useless as it is, I'm sorry I killed your kin. But I warn you: If we meet again I will have off your pretty head if need be."

He reined Demon round and rode off at a snow-slowed but steady pace, keeping a wary eye on the dark wood to his left. If this "sacred land" was the dark wood of Oxenglass, then Death was indeed close by.

And Rorc was that much closer to the inhuman Scourge he sought.

The woman shouted something after him in her necromantic tongue. Eerie echoes chased her voice and shook sprinklings of snowflakes from tree branches.

He shrugged off her curses and rode on along the wood-line, his eyes alert for a good place to make camp before nightfall. The puny witch's curse did not trouble him. His birth was his black curse, and he lived every day under its long, relentless shadow.

II.

The wind suddenly and sharply changed. Now it blew out of the north, icy and carrying the scent of menace. Demon snorted and bobbed his noble equine head. A tremor ran through his withers. Rorc's hand instinctively touched the pommel of his sword and he pricked up his ears to catch any uncommon sound the blade-sharp wind might carry.

Dusk was upon the land and its spacious shroud of snow seemed to glow with ghostly light from some unseen world.

There! The unmistakable sound of wings beating frosty air. Big wings.

Rorc was turning in his saddle to look in the direction from which the sound came when the thing hit him with spiky talons and snatched him off his horse. The talons were embedded in the layers of furs and leather Rorc wore, and he hung like a beggar's bulky suit of rags from the winged creature's feet as they glided low over the ground.

He yanked his dagger from his belt and thrust it blindly upward. The dagger-point glanced off one of the flying thing's limbs. Rorc thrust once more, the point striking true and drawing a shrill screech. The creature lost its hold and Rorc fell facedown in snow.

He rolled onto his right side and saw his attacker beating its leathery wings to gain altitude for another pass at its unhorsed prey. Against the paling purple sky, it looked like a red lizard with wings, slightly smaller in stature than the average man.

And it was fantastically fast. Before Rorc could get to his feet and unsheathe his sword, the flying lizard was swooping down for another attack, curved talons extended.

Demon interposed himself between man and predator, and reared to his full height. It was too late for the flying reptile to alter its course. The upright horse hammered the winged creature with his fore-hooves and swatted it to the ground, where the thing beat its wings uselessly against the snow and screeched in distress.

Rorc pushed to his feet, drew his blade and hacked off the monster's pebble-domed head. Blood gushed from its vulture-like neck and rained on the snow. It flapped its wings once, twice more, and fell dead.

But its head still issued pathetic shrieks, its reptilian maw mincing snow.

Rorc raised his blade and split the head apart, silencing the thing for good.

"Damnable country, to spawn a devil like this one," Rorc said as he cleaned his blade in the snow.

Demon neighed and nodded.

"You did well, you ill-tempered beast," he said to his horse. He patted Demon's thick neck; the horse snapped his teeth at Rorc's arm and would've taken a sizeable bite out of him had not Rorc been expecting the move and drawn his hand away. Rorc chuckled, and then said, "You're getting slow, old fellow."

Demon bared his teeth in a threatening grin.

Rorc walked a little way into the trees, found a deadfall, gathered firewood and soon had a campfire burning. Then he stripped naked to the waist, flung his long ropy war-braid over his shoulder and craned his neck to examine the talon wounds. They did not appear too deep, as his layers of furs had borne the brunt of the attack. Nevertheless, he cauterized with a red-hot ember of a tree branch the three wounds he could see. He ground his teeth against the pain. The stench of burning flesh made Demon restless, and he stamped hooves in the snow as if to express concern that his two-legged companion might be addle-brained.

The frigid night air took only a little of the burn from Rorc's back. He clothed his upper body again, and then dragged the dead winged creature into the wood and left it there to freeze and eventually rot come the next thaw. He tossed the thing's sundered head into the fire, where it sizzled long after its eyeballs exploded.

Wolves howled in the distance as Rorc bedded down by the fire and wrapped himself in extra furs. He gave himself to sleep and dreamt of the elusive Scourge that walked on two legs.

III.

Rorc awoke to a clamorous din echoing from snow-laden trees. He stood, sword in hand, and listened intently to the bestial yelps, growls and human shouts, judging that the commotion was taking place deep in the dark wood.

Wolf hunters, he surmised. The pelts of wolves drew a handsome price in the marketplaces to the south, where it was commonly believed that the pizzle and balls of the male wolf increased the sexual prowess of any man who ate them raw. The witch with the sapphire-blue eyes would surely be enraged by this slaughter and might, as a result, act recklessly. If the wolf hunters caught her, they would each take his turn at her loins before slitting her pretty throat and leaving her to die in the snowy wood.

He briefly considered picking the hunters off with arrows shot from concealment, skinning the wolves, and taking the pelts for himself, but he dismissed the idea as impractical. His hunt for the Scourge on Two Legs took precedence over any money-making scheme. If his eventual confrontation didn't go Rorc's way, he would have no need for money on his journey to the Underland of the Dead.

He saddled Demon and rode on, the din of the slaughter dying away in his wake.

Though the invisible sun was only on the first leg of its journey toward night, the sky was thickly overcast, ominous with promise of more snow. The biting cold and clammy mist gave Rorc the illusion of riding through a vast mountain of half-melted ice. He should not have been much surprised if he and his steed suddenly solidified in cruel sculptures of frozen flesh.

The gray day grew prematurely dark. Snow began to fall. Soon he was riding blindly into the worst snowstorm he'd ever seen. If the mammoth wood of Oxenglass was still there on his left, he could no longer see it. Demon plodded on, snorting plumes of smoke from his nostrils. Rorc shuddered against the cold and huddled deeper into his layers of leather and fur.

The north wind grew fiercer, howling in his face like an enraged cold-blooded beast. Snow mixed with ice stung his raw cheeks. Demon all at once halted and shook his head as if in disgust. Rorc had learned to place full trust in the horse's instincts. If Demon sensed danger ahead or if he judged the conditions too treacherous for moving ahead blindly, Rorc knew better than to try to press the animal onward. He patted Demon's neck and said, "Right, then. We wait."

Rorc dismounted and huddled beneath the makeshift shelter of the horse's belly. "Don't even think about pissing on me," he said, only half in jest.

The beast snorted contemptuously. His stomach rumbled and then he blew a great fart.

Soon Rorc was dozing and dreaming of sunny skies and flowered meadows. But hidden within the tall grass and green stalks were slithering serpents with venomous fangs, belly-crawling toward him with evil intent. He came awake with a jolt as one of the dream-serpents sank fangs into his leg.

The snowstorm had abated while he slept. Flurries swirled in dwindling wind. The immense forest was visible again, colossal trees standing like the wall of a camouflaged fortress. Rorc climbed out from under the horse, shook snow off his shoulders and head, brushed snow from the saddle and then mounted up and rode on.

He'd only gone a short distance when he came upon an injured wolf lying in the snow. The she-wolf's fur was almost as white as the snow, but its left hind leg was bloodied by the fractured bone that had broken through the skin and poked out like a shiny knob. When the wounded wolf saw the approaching horse and rider, she began to crawl through the snow in a futile attempt to escape. She glanced back at Rorc with sapphire-blue eyes.

Just then, two figures emerged from the trees and high-stepped through the snow toward the she-wolf. Wolf hunters, one armed with bow-and-arrow and the other with a long spear.

Rorc rode to a halt between the hunters and their wound prey.

"Hold," he said, his voice deep and commanding. "This wolf is mine."

"*Yours*," mocked the taller hunter, an ugly smirk on his bearded face.

"Ride on, horseman," said the other, "if you want to see sundown. This is Lord Oxenglass's land and you're trespassing. By rights, we could kill you where you sit and take that brute of a horse."

Rorc grinned, baring his teeth in naked scorn. He said, "Come on, then. This black behemoth is yours for the taking. All you have to do is kill me and tame the monster with pretty words and warm kisses. On his arse."

Demon snorted and danced restlessly. The she-wolf whimpered, then growled.

The tall man brought up his longbow and drew back his bowstring but before he could aim his arrow, Rorc pulled his throwing knife from his belt and hurled it at the bowman. Like sentient steel, the blade buried itself in the man's throat. The man's bow went slack and he dropped to his knees, clutching at his throat with both hands, gurgling loudly.

The spearman made the mistake of staring too long at his dying companion before raising his spear and cocking his arm for the throw. Rorc put heels to his horse and Demon burst forward in a hard, snow-kicking gallop as Rorc unsheathed his sword and raised it over his shoulder.

The spear rushed past Rorc's left ear an instant before he slashed the sword downward and hacked off the hunter's extended arm at the shoulder. Blood arced from the man's stump and pattered on the snow, but he remained on his feet, staring down at his severed arm.

Rorc reined Demon round in a tight circle and sliced off the spearman's head with one powerful stroke. The head fell facedown in the snow. A fount of blood gushing from the neck, the spearman's body remained standing, held in place by knee-deep snow. Rorc pushed the headless corpse backward onto the snow-crusted ground with his sword point, and then dismounted to tend to the she-wolf. Up close, it was the biggest wolf he'd ever seen.

"Is that you, witch?" he asked. As he'd never seen a wolf with such striking blue eyes, he was all but certain this was the shape-shifter lying injured before him. "Be easy now. I'm going to help you. I can set that leg if you'll let me."

The she-wolf growled, then whimpered, regarding him warily.

Rorc drew his dagger. "Bite down on the handle while I fix your leg. Bite me and I'll leave you to starve."

He held the dagger in front of her mouth. Reluctantly, she clamped her teeth on the dagger's handle and looked away as if ashamed.

"This will hurt. But I'll do it quickly." He knelt in the snow and took the broken leg in both hands. "Right, then. Here we go."

With strong hands he snapped the broken leg back into place. The she-wolf growled and bit down harder on the pommel.

"Good girl," he said. "Now rest easy while I find wood for a splint."

She glanced over her shoulder and fixed him with a cold stare. Her blue eyes were swimming in tears.

IV.

With the mammoth trees forming a windbreak, Rorc dug a firepit in the small clearing and cooked an unusually large hare he'd felled with an arrow. He'd offered the she-wolf a portion of uncooked meat but she refused it. She lay close to the crackling fire, unafraid of the flames or of the man who'd set her leg.

He drank the last of his wineskin's contents, and as it often did, the fermented spirits loosened his tongue and he talked to the wolf.

"I am called Rorc, short for Rorculus-ab-null. I was born nine and twenty years ago on Hag Mountain, the only human ever born on that mystical mount. My mother was like you, a necromancer—or so I was told when I was a sprout. As soon as she birthed me, she gave me away to a passing band of godless barbarians from the south. A wet-nurse raised me until I was old enough to fight, and then the Master of Arms trained me in the ways of combat." He paused long enough to chuckle. "They say my father was a devil my mother conjured for some dark purpose and that I was cursed from birth. I don't doubt it. Nor do I much care. We're all cursed with life, eh witch?"

The she-wolf studied him with her wintry eyes. He felt as if she were looking deep into his heart.

"Can you not change back to your womanly form?" he asked. "I feel the fool, talking so to a wolf. No? Is it because of your injury?"

He shrugged. "No matter. With enough wine in my belly, I'd talk to a stone. And you *are* the handsomest wolf I've ever laid eyes upon."

The meager firelight cast capering shadows on the massive tree trunks surrounding the camp, making Rorc uneasy. Ordinarily, he didn't fear shadows, but there was nothing ordinary about this ancient forest, which was now the province of Lord Oxenglass, a ruthless man said to be in league with various denizens of darkness and a gaggle of Underland devils.

He glanced at his horse. Demon was ever sensitive to harbingers of hazard, but now the great black steed stood at ease at the foot of a giant tree, so Rorc went on with the raw tale of his life. He'd never bothered to tell it to anyone before, but something about this she-wolf compelled him to speak it. Was the blue-eyed bitch working some spell on him?

"I grew into a lanky lad, tall and sinewy, so the stout tribesmen often misjudged my fighting abilities, and not a one of them ever beat me. They took to saying I got my unnatural strength from the dark magic that spawned me. Maybe so." Rorc shrugged. "All I know is I've never been bested in battle."

The wind moaned in the trees. A thousand baritone banshees might've been singing from a thousand twisted branches. Rorc shivered and went on with his tale.

"When I was ten and six, I deflowered the chieftain's daughter. It was a foolhardy thing to do, as she was promised in marriage to the chieftain of another tribe. By rights, they could've killed me on the spot. Instead, they chained me to a barmy bear and banished me to the wilderness. A great black bear, it was, feeble-brained, mean and unpredictable. The beast had once been used for the chieftain's amusement, trained to caper and dance and act the fool in a silly hat, but then the damned thing danced itself into madness, so rather than kill it for the bearskin, they chained us together and sent us away, sure the bear would eventually make feast of me or bat me about for its own amusement till my guts fell out.

"For three days and nights the bear dragged me along as it ranged madly through the wood. It seemed to have no interest in me, and I began to think I would starve to death rather than be eaten. But then the bastard finally took notice of me and decided to have me for supper. With only twenty feet of chain between us, there was no way I could outrun him for long. He was as tireless as he was mad and hungry. So there it was: I had to fight him to the death. I figured my only chance was to limit his range of motion and hamper his attack. I ran round and round a tree to shorten the chain and hold him fast to it, leaving just enough lengths of chain to wrap round his throat and choke the life from him. My tactic confused him and I was able to come round the tree, jump on his back and slip the chain over his head and round his thick neck. It took all my strength and much time, but I finally killed him.

"Then I had a new problem. Chained to a dead bear, I would die of thirst because he was too heavy to drag. There was only one way to free myself. I had to chew off all the flesh and fur from his leg and then break the bone against the tree in order to slip the chain off. This I did. It took all of a day and part of a night. I ate, then puked, ate and puked some more, until I'd eaten my way to freedom. I was sick for days after."

The she-wolf watched him closely. He was sure she understood his words. And now he was all but certain that she was drawing his story from him by means of dark magic. He *had* to go on with it, though he wanted to slip under a pile of furs and sleep till morn.

"A banished monk from the east found me sickened nigh unto death, and nursed me back to health. I learned later that Haruki had been exiled from his monastery for delving into forbidden magicks. It was he who taught me to read and write and think like a man of reason. He also taught me how to kill a man with my little finger and how to creep unseen with a countenance of darkest night. For a froggy little man with webbed fingers and toes, he moved like a cat. He'd forsaken his devotion to the god of his monastic brothers in order to truck with the Old Ones of the frozen seas of the Far North. He told me these old gods came from beyond the stars and would soon rise again to rule the world. His conviction was so strong that I believed him. But he died of fasting and left me to wander alone.

"It was he who told me of the Scourge on Two Legs and charged me with killing it. He said I was bound to it by birth and that I had to be the one to kill it. I vowed to do it, and my many years of hunting it have brought me here. The Oracle of Black Cave said I would find the Scourge at the end of Oxenglass Wood, but the albino bitch would not predict the outcome. No matter. I will kill it even if I have to die doing it. I may, as you say, be a barbarian, but my oath is gold."

V.

Two simultaneous sounds summoned him from sleep: Demon neighing and the she-wolf snarling.

Rorc threw off his bedding of furs and sprang to his feet with sword in hand. The firepit was aglow with dying embers. A half-moon high in the crisp night sky cast its ghostly light through the trees and upon the snow. He ground his teeth; he squinted to sharpen his eyesight. If there was someone or something creeping up on him, he couldn't see it.

Demon's hooves restlessly crunched snow. Her ears laid back, the wolf-witch growled louder as she stared into the trees.

She had come to him in his dream, slipped under the covers and curled, naked, against him. She'd been in human form and the contact with her flesh had at once aroused him. Even now, the steel in his loins felt as strong as the steel in his hand. The unseen threat in the dark wood did not diminish his arousal, which somehow sharpened his senses to a single rigid point and…there! At last he saw them shambling out of the trees.

Six tall figures in black suits of armor, three with battleaxes and three with deadly warhammers. The armor creaked and clattered as they advanced.

For the first time ever, Rorc's brutish horse seemed afraid; he felt the fear coming off the animal like frigid air from the frozen northlands. The she-wolf, however, did not back down from the advancing figures in black armor. She crouched low to the ground, her splint half-submerged in snow, and snarled with increased fury. Her blue eyes shone eerily in the moonlight.

Using a martial technique the banished monk from the east had taught him, Rorc visualized a Circle of Mayhem with himself in its center. When his adversaries entered the imaginary circle, he would launch his attack and his sword's blade would sweep the circle with lightning speed, slowing his foes' advance and giving him the advantage of surprise against uneven odds. He knew and accepted that he might very well die here. Death ruled the Circle of Mayhem. The men in black armor were taller than he, and likely stronger, but Rorc was determined to fill the circle with his slashing, flying blade. "Out of one blade, many," Haruki had taught him.

So as soon as the armored warriors entered the circle, Rorc raised his sword in a two-handed grip, gave a war-cry and attacked. The war-cry should've sounded like the cry of a hawk, but what came out was more like the howl of a wolf. Though this startled him, he pressed his attack in a blur of speed and struck each of the six armored warriors a single blow. Much to his amazement, two of them immediately fell. But one of the others swung his warhammer squarely at Rorc's head.

He ducked and the hammerhead brushed the top of his head, taking a few hanks of hair with it. The hammer-swing exposed his assailant's belly as a tempting target and Rorc plunged the sword through the flimsy armor and into the man's gut. The man twisted and fell, taking Rorc's sword with him.

Divested of his weapon, Rorc grabbed the dropped warhammer and went on the attack with it, swinging it with all his sinewy strength at the helmed head of the warrior closest to him. The man's head flew off his shoulders and landed in the snow with a muffled thud. The force of the blow had knocked the helm's visor off, and Rorc saw that the face inside the helmet was not human. Its eyes were made of finely spun filaments of green leaves, glistening with dewy film. Twisted vines of dark wood formed its cheeks and forehead. Its nose was a rough knot of pine bark. Rorc saw, too, that the armor was not metal but black wood. He had no doubt that these creatures had been fashioned from the dark forest by sorcery. But by whom?

Another of the wood-men swung his warhammer at Demon, barely missing the horse's head. Incensed enough to overcome his fear of dark magic, Demon reared up and kicked his attacker to the ground and then trampled it.

The she-wolf leapt at one of them and knocked it on its back. She tore into its throat with her wicked teeth, drawing forth black sap instead of blood.

Rorc rounded on the remaining combatant and knocked its legs out from under it with the heavy warhammer. Then he planted a foot on its chest and said, "If you have a voice, speak and tell me who made you. Remain silent and I will turn you to pulpwood."

A man's voice boomed from the trees: "*I* made him. And I made you too."

VI.

"Show yourself, sorcerer," Rorc said to the unseen speaker.

A tall figure in a black hooded cloak stepped into the clearing. His face was stark white in the moonlight. His lips curled into a thin smile. His eyes reflected no light.

The she-wolf whined as if in fright.

Demon dropped a pile of horse apples.

"Who *are* you?" Rorc asked.

The tall man said, "I believe you call me the Scourge on Two Legs. But you may call me *Father*." He chuckled. It sounded like dry leaves blowing across cold stone. "Haruki taught you well, lad. Unfortunately, he did not teach you true."

"Why would I call you *Father*?"

"Because I fucked the bitch who birthed you. She summoned a lesser demon and I came in its stead. You are of my seed."

"You lie!"

"Do I? Or do you lie to yourself?" Again the man laughed. Again dead leaves scraped stone. "Son of the Scourge. I rather like the sound of that. Don't you?"

Rorc ground his teeth.

The man said, "You shall be my whip-hand, my son, when I send you forth to punish the world of men for their fealty to false gods."

"I'd sooner die than serve you."

"That is your choice to make. But be advised, your death will last aeons. You will suffer interminably."

"I don't know who you are, but you're not the Scourge. You look like an ordinary human to me."

"Your eyes deceive. And your heart is tainted by misguided hate. I am he, the one you vowed to destroy."

"If you are so determined to die, then I will oblige you." Rorc moved toward the man and cocked the warhammer over his shoulder.

The man held up a hand. Rorc froze, unable to move; he felt as if the cloaked figure held his entire being in the palm of his death-pale hand.

"Your next actions will be of great consequence," said the man. "You should not undertake them under any misapprehension. Behold."

The man raised both arms over his head and whispered words Rorc couldn't understand. The giant tress behind the man in the cloak fell away to nothingness. Where the dark wood had stood was now an endless abyss. It looked as if the earth had simply broken off and drifted away into space.

The she-wolf began to howl mournfully.

"I am the Scourge at the End of the World," the man said. "You cannot destroy me. If you try, you will do great harm to yourself. Feel the truth of my words. Your mad mother gave you away while I was translated to another realm, and you ended up with Haruki, servant and spawn of the Old Ones from a distant star. They fancy themselves gods and intend to infest this earth with a hybrid race of fish-men. I will not let this happen. I—and you—must punish and subjugate the human race to save it from these star-flung interlopers who would be gods. Know you this: I am neither human nor inhuman, and you are my offspring. You *must* serve me. Or else become degenerate—a barbarous man-thing with shrunken soul. Or perhaps the wayward ghost of a rotting corpse."

The Scourge—there was no longer any question of his identity—waved his right hand and Rorc's power of movement returned.

"I have sworn to kill you," said Rorc, grinding his teeth. "My word is gold."

"Your word is shit. But go ahead, if you must. Hammer me into oblivion."

Rorc obliged. He swung the great warhammer down on the cloaked man's head. He hammered and hammered, pounding the man into the snow-crusted earth until there was nothing left but crushed bones and pulped gore.

Overcome with fatigue, Rorc collapsed. The world spun round his throbbing head, the half-moon and scattered stars, unmoored from the predawn sky, sank into the abyss.

Then the ground beneath the ghastly remains of the Scourge suddenly erupted and bloodied vines shot up out of the fouled earth, twisting and twining about one another like red muscle knitting to bone. The Scourge reconstituted itself as a hideous giant with no skin over its raw musculature. Its face was hawk-like and fierce, its black eyes too terrifying to gaze upon.

"You have too much of the maternal madwoman in you," the Scourge said in a slithery voice. He reached down with fingers long and skeletal like bare tree branches and pressed their sharp tips into Rorc's skull. "Die, then. Your ghost will chastise mortals with their own fears, so even in death you will serve me."

Great leathery wings unfolded from the Scourge's back and it flew lazily off into the void at the edge of the world.

Rorc lay on his back and waited for Death to take him.

The she-wolf stood over him and licked his blood-spattered face. Rorc shut his eyes, surrendering to the ministrations of her rough tongue.

When he opened his eyes again, he was looking into the beautiful face of the woman with sapphire-blue eyes. She was naked, her skin white but furless. She stripped his clothes off him; he shivered against the cold.

"If you wish to live," she said, "then suck." She offered one of her six teats.

He took the nipple into his mouth and sucked the breast dry of its honeyed fluid; she thrust the next teat into his mouth. She suckled him until her many breasts were drained of their seductive elixir. He fell into a deep sleep.

Sated and restored to robust health, Rorc awoke. He'd never felt more vibrantly alive. The woman had wrapped herself in furs and now stood above him. When he tried to speak and thank her for saving his life, all he could do was growl. His tongue lolled out to taste the crisply delicious air.

The woman smiled down at him. She scratched the fur behind his long ears.

He tried to return her smile, but couldn't, so he sat down to lick his balls.

RANDY CHANDLER is the author of the novels *Dime De-
tective, Daemon of the Dark Wood, HELLz BELLz,* and *Stolen
Roads.* He also co-authored *Duet For the Devil* with t. Winter-
Damon (God rest his soul). Randy's collection of short stories
is *Devils, Death & Dark Wonders.* He is the Associate Editor of
Red Room Press and co-editor of *Year's Best Hardcore Horror.*

Randy has been an indie magazine editor/publisher, a freelance book
reviewer, a mental health worker, a gas-pump jockey, an ambulance
attendant, a soldier in Vietnam, and a funeral home flunky. He often
haunts fields of carnage where angels and devils do battle.

www.ingramcontent.com/pod-product-compliance
Lightning Source LLC
Chambersburg PA
CBHW070935250626
47159CB00009B/3260